Hope you
enjoy.
Caroline
19.7.23.
x .

CW00551321

Symbols
of the
Future

Caroline Read

novum  pro

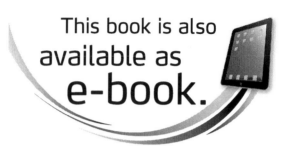

This book is also
available as
e-book.

www.novum-publishing.co.uk

© 2016 novum publishing

ISBN 978-3-99048-472-2
Editor: Louise Darvid
Cover photo:
Vasyl Duda | Dreamstime.com
Cover design, layout & typesetting:
novum publishing

www.novum-publishing.co.uk

Prologue

Peace in the Middle East had been celebrated after many years of human sacrifice and suffering. Many had asked if the death toll had really been worth the centuries of fighting, loss of life and all the sorrow that had ensued. Eventually, the realisation dawned that there could be no winners, only losers, whatever creed. Those leaders which had reigned with fear and violence had long since been eradicated and the climate of the world had changed, some would say, beyond recognition over the last 50 years. Egypt was no longer the desert-like country that it used to be in the last century and of which the peoples of the late 1900s would remember. Rainfall had increased dramatically and desert land was fast disappearing. Rivers now flowed past the great pyramids and the Sphinx was surrounded by a vast lake, in some parts as deep as a small ocean. Sadly these holy lands which had been renowned for their structural wonders, where tales of early miracles and intelligent life had been born, were now of little interest. They had once been at the heart of many archaeological expeditions, evoking thought and theories that perhaps mysterious beings may have once inhabited the Earth and built these wondrous structures, maybe even inspiring the growth and evolution of our ancient ancestors.

Certainly climatically, the changes were very profound and some islands that had once flourished and supported a significant eco system to give life to human and the animal populations had disappeared under water, lost forever. Major devastation had occurred decades ago, causing astronomical changes for mankind. Technology, which had been growing steadily until that point, was forced through necessity to advance at a greater pace to another level and in this transition came the birth of the Transnanite Regenerating Intelligence Governing Over Mankind;

generally referred to as T.R.I.G.O.M. ... This in turn marked the beginning of the greatest change the Earth and its inhabitants could ever imagine possible but perhaps not even the most advanced technology would be its saviour and only ancient knowledge could truly ensure the continuation of Mankind.

Chapter One

Torri looked up at the night sky and as ever was in awe of the vastness of the universe. She had always appreciated the beauty of the many constellations of twinkling stars. Although she knew that they were millions of miles away, they looked so bright and vibrant, almost as if they were there to light the way to some secret place. It was here on the banks of the Nile, alone on her favourite spot by the shimmering light of the Egyptian moon that she found time to reflect. It was when she was here more than anywhere else that she felt the loss of her grandfather, she missed him so much. His protective arms around her whenever she needed comfort; his words of wisdom, whenever she felt lost. Oh she missed him so much. She had been only fifteen when he had passed, but she had known that it was going to happen, she had seen it in one of her many visions. It had come to her one evening, quickly and without warning, as they always did. She had been unable to contain her tears but knew that she could do nothing to prevent what must be. She had reached the tender age of three when these visions had first started and as a young child she had been frightened and bewildered, not understanding what was happening. They were so vivid that many times she felt that she was physically there, witnessing whatever event was being shown to her. At first she had not been able to tell anyone, in fear that she would be ridiculed or even that she would get into trouble. Her grandfather had been the first person she had found the courage to confide in with the hope that he would make things better as he always did. He, more than anyone had understood her and accepted her "gift" as he explained it to her, which had made her love him even more. He had never judged her or lost his patience; her kind gentle grandfather had given

7

her the precious gift of his unconditional love. Reflecting back now and although at the time it hadn't seemed strange that he had shown no surprise at her revelation, she was sure that he too had a gift and so he had been able to understand her completely. He had been her guiding star, helping her along, what started out as a rocky path, before she was able to finally accept her "gift". A gift that sometimes made her feel alone and vulnerable, she felt different, even from her own mother and father but even at her loneliest times she could feel her destiny beckoning and it gave her hope. Spiritualism was nothing new and it had been fairly widespread and accepted many years ago but now, not many people actually practised it or made it common knowledge that they had such a gift. Torri believed that perhaps it was not looked too kindly on by the T.R.I.G.O.M. board, but after all it was not controllable. She often had an overwhelming feeling that her destiny was connected to her gift and during some of her visions, her conscious mind faded from reality so that she was actually in the place and time of the event that she was being shown, feeling, hearing; all her senses alive with the moment. It was not uncommon for her to feel weak and nauseous for some time after but she had learned how to cope and tried to live her life as normally as possible. Now, years later and after having had many experiences of this kind, she knew that whatever role she had in the future it would take all of her courage and faith but that she was becoming stronger and stronger and so she had learned not to be frightened; instead she embraced her gift, knowing that one day it would be needed.

Chapter Two

Most of her childhood education, as with all children of her age, had been spent alone in her computer room, her parents providing her only guidance but at the age of eight she had been overjoyed when she had found out that she had been chosen by the T.R.I.G.O.M. learning council to be one of a select few children to be given an opportunity to attend an experimental learning class. This had been set up on a trial basis to assess whether or not physical activity could promote a higher level of learning. She was so excited that instead of being alone by the computer, she would actually get the chance to meet and interact with other children. Although her parents had not seemed too keen on this idea at first, she had managed to persuade them to let her try it. Torri secretly thought that they had consented in the end to get some peace from her constant chatter. She hadn't been able to stop talking about it and had bombarded them with pleas to let her go. She was not the usual quiet child of the time and frustrated her parents by her insatiable appetite to learn. She would always be asking questions if there was something that she didn't understand and added to her liking for the outdoors her parents had become very worried that she wouldn't fit into the society created by T.R.I.G.O.M. They just could not understand her and where possible they tried to discourage her outdoor activities so that attention would not be drawn to them. She was so thankful that they had allowed her to go to these classes and, whatever their reasons, she had felt overjoyed and couldn't wait to tell her beloved grandfather that they had finally said yes. She knew that he would be pleased for her.

This opportunity had given her the chance to make friends with other children of her own age, share their interests and play together, which was now a thing of the past. She had been nervous on her first day but as soon as she entered the learning room her nerves disappeared being replaced with excitement, expectations and an eagerness to learn. She loved the days when she attended these classes and made many friends but she had also experienced first-hand, childish cruelty and adult prejudice when her "gift" became common knowledge. Many times she had come home full of the things that she had learned and eagerly talking about her friends but there had been days when she came home in tears after being teased by a fellow classmate or rebuked by one of the adult overseers. The adults were less understanding of her and who didn't seem to have much time for this strange child, as some of them cruelly thought of her. Once again her grandfather had always been there with a hug and words of reassurance, making everything better. Now at twenty-four she was able to look back and cherish the times that they had spent together, reflecting upon his wise words which had always given her so much courage. Her other comfort and whom she had been able to confide in had been her friend who she had met on her first day at her learning class all those years ago. She had arrived with her brother, a quiet boy prone to sulking and who didn't seem to like the friendship that she had formed with his sister. He always seemed so jealous and possessive, Torri had not liked him at all but her friendship with his sister had prospered and grown even so.

It had been such a sad day for Torri when she had been told that her classes were to end. The learning board had not liked the interaction classes which encouraged students to be active and to form physical friendships which could not always be controlled. They preferred instead to revert back to the individual learning that T.R.I.G.O.M. provided where physical interaction was not necessary and control was easier, sat in a solitary learning room. The experiment had not met with their expectations, they had added no further explanations and all facilities had been withdrawn.

However, their friendship had lasted long after the learning classes had ceased, their bond strengthened and nurtured by many long chats through the computer links. Torri had been so upset to say goodbye to her friend, there was a sadness about her but she had not had any visions or premonitions about her future which was unusual, only a strong sense that they both needed a friend and confidante. She had been frantic with worry when their communication had suddenly stopped and more than a little shocked that she had no idea why, even when she tried to draw on her own spiritual ability. Her only comfort was that she knew she was alive to fulfil her own destiny and that one day their paths would meet again.

ENGLAND – 2183

The vehicle seemed to come from nowhere … Joshua had been in a world of his own; full of excitement having just left the academy, such a rarity these days to attend a meeting, rather than alone and through the computer. Although great advancements had been made in the last decade with special eye chips implanted at birth which, when activated enabled the viewer to experience amazing visual 3D images, it was still a poor second to actually being at a venue physically and being able to embrace the atmosphere it generated. To hear someone talking provoked feeling and an intensity that a computer link, no matter how advanced, just could not create. He had been enthralled by the words of the professor, whom he had greatly admired since his tutorial days and whose works in the computer library system had first inspired him to pursue his interest in ancient history. Although not a widely popular subject in this modern society or even greatly encouraged as it involved a good deal of physical activities, he had not been deterred by the negativity of others in his choice to pursue this path of learning. It had paid off as he was now well on his way to becoming a respected researcher and philosopher in this field with his debates of ancient relics and symbols in the modern world and their possible significance to the future. His papers exploring his theories on ancient artefacts investigated the authenticity of many of these discoveries. He had even managed to get some of his writings accepted into the computer library system and this was indeed a great achievement for someone so young. They had created interest within the history section, often used as references or chosen topics by the monthly debating groups. These were groups of people from all over the world, linked by the holographic conferencing system, who liked to put forward or discuss issues, usually on a monthly basis. These groups were initially formed and promoted to help when great cultural and technical changes had taken place, it was a way of communication, helping and encouraging people to attain acceptance in a changing world. Now, however, it was more of a social gathering to practise conversational arts and strengthen friendship links although they were still monitored closely by T.R.I.G.O.M.

"These artefacts bring us knowledge to embrace and hold the key to understanding our past but what of our future?" He was mulling over the meaning of the professor's words when the vehicle hit. He hadn't been concentrating on the road. All vehicles were strictly controlled by T.R.I.G.O.M. and any form of accident or incident happened very rarely. Pedestrians, who were few and far between, would never pay too much attention to the roads or have any fear of a vehicle hitting them. The vehicles with their highly adapted scanners and programs should have made it impossible for accidents to happen. The impact was sudden, followed by a sharp pain down his right hand side and a searing pain in his head. He was fading in and out of consciousness, but through the black mist that kept engulfing him, he saw a man staring down at him as he lay badly injured and unable to move; his piercing blue eyes showing no emotion. The events that followed were hazy but he vaguely remembered hearing panicked voices shouting as emergency vehicles approached. He thought the approaching vehicles had made the man jump but he couldn't be sure and after closing his eyes for a moment again, the man had disappeared. Perhaps it was a figment of his imagination brought on by shock and pain. Just before he completely passed out he saw the blue emergency Air Disc land and felt himself being lifted up.

Chapter Three

The computer's emergency M.I.R. (Medical Intelligence Robot) had worked quickly and tirelessly to revive Joshua and just on the last attempt to revive him, his heart started to beat. The monitor's sudden bleep drew relieved looks by the crash team technicians, who had been observing on the monitoring screens. They were there to ensure that the computer systems were functioning correctly. Human doctors still worked in the hospitals, but their role had evolved into a more technical supervisory one, with computers taking over the main work load, performing the day to day routine work and all of the intricate operations.

Human contact with patients had been restricted within all hospitals to reduce the risk of infections. This had come into force in the latter part of 2070, after the outbreak of an extremely voracious virus which had affected 30 % of the world's human population. Now, cleanliness was of the highest level and monitored closely by the main frame computer which would automatically shut off any contaminated areas if detected. Appearance enhancing procedures accounted for the majority of patients in hospitals, reflecting both the vast medical advancements which had been made regarding major illnesses but sadly reflecting a regression of the human race, due to vanity and materialistic obsessions. In the past, hospitals had been sued for large sums of money when the old monetary systems existed, by patients recovering from these procedures, when the risk of infection was high, causing deformities and fatalities. Ironically, money had been the underlying source of infection as cleanliness and the wellbeing of people within the hospitals had suffered because of lack of funding and expenditure; the importance put on cost values above all else. This at least had been eradicated and money was of no importance.

After the relief of his resuscitation, Joshua was now ready to be transferred to the recovery room and in accordance to customary procedures; this is where he would be left until he regained consciousness. After a few hours his eyes opened slowly, the light of the room causing him pain as he tried to focus on his surroundings. He was in a small bright room which smelt of disinfectant with an odd sound which he couldn't place. Nurses had long been replaced with artificial intelligence units, linked to the main frame computer which controlled the main support functions of this modern society. The sound he couldn't place was the constant hum of the computer, usually a sound that was so low that people did not realise it was there. Maybe it was because he had been unconscious for so long and had not been able to hear the humming noise but it now appeared to be getting louder and his head started to thump with the sound. He tried to open his eyes again but the brightness of the room intensified the pain in his head. The computer, which was monitoring his vital signs, detected his eye movement, instantly recognising the pain reaction to the bright light and within a split second the blinds had closed automatically, dimming the light to a softer level, relieving some of his discomfort. The bed started to adjust itself to a partial sitting position, the computer automatically executing its programme to ensure the patient has the highest level of comfort and relief. Spontaneously, a message had been generated notifying the Doctors that the patient had regained consciousness. Josh wanted to speak, but his mouth felt so dry, he started to panic. Once again the computer acted immediately and he felt his throat being sprayed with a fine mist of water administered from the tubes that he was attached to. Every need was catered for, the computer linked to him by very fine silvery optic strands which had become a temporary part of his body. He slowly started to remember who he was and vaguely recalled the vehicle heading towards him, he had thought intentionally and then he could remember nothing else. As he became more aware of his surroundings, a distant dream of a bright light filled his mind but then a sharp pain in his right arm dispelled all other thoughts. As he was now in a sitting position, he could see that his arm was in the break tube, his bones being mended by the "repair machine," he knew that it would not be long before his broken arm would be mended. Just then a man appeared wearing a white coat and smiled at Joshua. Although this was unusual for any human contact, Joshua was feeling somewhat disorientated and just looked at the man as he approached, not even wondering why he was in his room. This small white haired man smiled warmly at him and although by now Joshua had started to feel very light headed and sick he noticed that the man was looking at his arm. The room had started spinning and a hazy mist was covering his vision. He was beginning to feel very uncomfortable. Just before Josh passed out again, he thought he felt the man touch his arm; it started to tingle. The mist got thicker before his eyes; he couldn't see anymore. His arm started to burn slightly and then darkness took over. He was once again drifting in and out of consciousness, uncertain of what was reality. He thought he heard a soft voice whispering his name, a strange vibration flowing through his body as he thought he could see shadowy silhouettes in the distance. Then a bright light in the distance seemed to draw him near. In this dream-like state he felt very much alive. He thought he heard a distant voice, so soft that at first he thought it was music but then he heard, "Joshua you have work to do so that we all may have hope again for the future." Joshua didn't feel afraid, but strangely calmed by this voice which instilled an odd feeling of recognition which he couldn't quite place.

"Where am I?" He knew he had not actually uttered the words but that he had said them and they had been heard and understood.

"You are safe, in a place that you know but can't remember. The old order is soon to change and so we must prepare for the new. You will need to travel to fulfil your chosen path and amongst the artefacts you will learn the reason of your existence through one who is as special as you. Do not be afraid you will know what to do but now you will return back along the bridge of light, to the heavy burden which is your physical body."

Joshua had felt so free and as light as a feather then suddenly it was like a weight pushing him back, which he could not stop. He wanted to go further into the light but knew that this could not be and in that one instant everything was clear and he understood, then darkness enveloped him again and this knowledge had returned to the recesses of his mind which he could not access.

Chapter Four

Torri got up from her favourite place by the Nile to return home. The night air had become cool and she shivered slightly as she wrapped her shawl tighter around her shoulders. She had been slightly troubled by a sudden image of a young man in a hospital bed. As she saw him lying there a sharp shooting pain in her right arm made her jump, such was the force of the pain. The face was of a stranger but she felt she knew him. She had felt a wave of love engulf her at this strange recognition followed by panic which she couldn't explain. Having tried to make sense of this vision and her feelings, she had decided that she was tired and it was time to go. Time, as ever, had flown and she had not been aware of the lateness of the hour. Time seemed to pass more quickly for everyone nowadays and she wasn't sure if this was just imagination or if it was a scientific fact and the Earth was in some way changing its rotation, perhaps in preparation of things to come! She was surprised at these thoughts; were they hers or was it perhaps part of a premonition or vision yet to come? Her head full of past and future contemplations, she was glad to reach her bed …

It had now been a couple of weeks since Joshua had been released from the hospital but he had not felt the same since the accident. He had become quiet and withdrawn, not being able to forget his experience. He became agitated and on edge for no reason, almost as if he felt he should be somewhere else or doing something different and it was getting frustrating. His arm ached a lot and it sometimes felt so hot he could barely touch it. The constant numbness followed by the sensation of pins and needles being pushed into his arm was more intensified at night preventing him from sleeping properly. Josh had always been a good sleeper. He cherished the fond memories of his mother taking great delight to tease his father whenever she could, telling everyone that Josh could sleep through anything; even the loudest volume that the computer could generate of his father's beloved Orchestral Music. His father loved all music with a passion, mostly preferring the old Operatic Music which was harder and harder to obtain or the new music compilations that T.R.I.G.O.M. supplied to everyone. His father had insisted on programming all varieties of music into the family computer which was timed to blast out every morning to wake the household, a cause thoroughly lost on Joshua as he always slept soundly, causing much laughter from his mother and great frustration from his father. This sleep deprivation was causing him some concern and even his work, which he loved, did nothing to lift him out of this dark mood. Learning of ancient civilisations and handling the precious artefacts usually brought him elation and wonder, but now other thoughts were beginning to cross his mind as he started to remember more details about his accident and the events afterwards. Whose was that soft voice? Did he imagine it? And lately the face of a young girl seemed to fill his thoughts. The accident itself troubled him. All vehicles were supposed to be controlled by T.R.I.G.O.M., so how did it happen? As he had been recovering in the hospital, he had time to think and ponder over the circumstances of his accident. Towards the end of his stay in hospital he had been visited by various medical staff in person, not just the robots attending. He had asked questions but everyone seemed to be a little vague and he got the feeling that he was being steered away from any form of investigation. Once he had got back home and had the use of his T.R.I.G.O.M. link he had wanted to initiate a full enquiry. T.R.I.G.O.M. would not give out any information and all he got back was that the details were classified and not obtainable. The more he thought about it the more frustrated he got, he was even thinking of making an appointment to see the council, something that nobody had ever done before to his knowledge. He was putting together his application to do just that when the telephone rang.

Chapter Five

"Hi, Josh, it's Patrick." Joshua smiled, recognising the Irish lilt as that of his old school pal. He had not heard from him for over a year but he had not thought much of it. It was his usual pattern, either falling for a vision of beauty, usually blonde and loud, or throwing himself into some project which would consume him completely.

"If it's not my long lost Irish Leprechaun," Josh jokingly answered. "Thought you had fallen off the face of the Earth, but as usual, like a bad penny …"

They both laughed, enjoying their special bond which never lessened, no matter how long the absence had been since they had last seen each other. Josh felt his spirits lifting almost immediately, the first time in days he had actually felt like his usual self, without that foreboding feeling and those troubled thoughts in his mind. "Hey, listen, Josh, got this job, researching in the Middle East, Egypt to be precise, a private commission, regarding some ancient symbols and some sort of predictions and possible ancient aliens. Probably a load of rubbish, but who did I think might like the challenge and even be remotely interested in the quest?" He was laughing now, knowing Josh only too well, he would want to snap his hands off for this chance. Patrick liked a good time, beer, sun and the odd Egyptian beauty but they both shared a passion for adventure and the love of ancient artefacts. He knew Josh's appetite for knowledge was unquenchable and his natural curiosity would be aroused so that he would want to know more about the commission that he spoke of. His love of ancient history, with its never ending mysteries would be too much for Josh to resist he was certain. Patrick needed Josh for this trip, without him it wasn't going to happen. Patrick had nerve and bravado but Josh had the imagination and knowledge to solve ancient mysteries or at least put a good theory together.

He had been right, even though Josh tried to control his excitement with a coolness and blasé response. "Well I am not really doing much at the moment and could do with a change, after the accident, life has been a bit dull so perhaps I might take you up on that."

"Pick you up at 8.30 tomorrow, my friend," Patrick responded.

"What, that quick? There's no way I will be ready in time."

"Eey be gorra, stop being a wuss." Patrick put on his comical Irish lingo which always made Josh laugh. "Throw a few things into a bag and you'll be set, see you tomorrow." With that Patrick put the phone down, a large grin covering his face, not giving Josh a chance to reply.

Josh was also smiling although with a hint of panic. He liked to be organised, well planned and certainly wasn't used to having to pack without having at least two days' notice and even that would be pushing it. It was, however, quite a nice feeling to be doing something spontaneous; it felt like a breath of fresh air. He had wanted to get away for some time, so this was the opportunity he had been waiting for, not planned, totally random.

He had managed to find his travel bag and as he started to throw a few things into it, his mind began to wonder about the reasons he was actually going to Egypt. His conversation with Patrick had been brief with little detail, usual for Patrick but was he imagining it or was there a kind of urgency in his voice? He wondered who it was that had commissioned this visit. Predictions, what was that all about? A glimmer of a memory and something about travelling, but the memory was vague and would not clear. So what of this project? Aliens? He found himself smiling at the thought. He had heard theories that the Earth had once been visited in ancient times, hence the cave drawings, with rumours of visits in later times. A few people had endeavoured to write books on the subject, even suggesting that some religious beliefs had stemmed from off worldly visitors which had then been incorporated into history in whatever form could be understood at that time. How would you describe a spaceship to people from an ancient time? A cloud in the sky? A burning ball of light? He thought that this hypothesis had been well covered before, so nothing new there, but what ancient symbols could there be that had not been fully investigated before? His interest was intensified and he couldn't help wondering who wanted to know. So many questions started to buzz through his head. Yes this is what he needed, a distraction from his dark thoughts, an interest, something to wet his appetite and stimulate his thoughts …

Chapter Six

Although not having slept for more than a few hours, Josh was up at six. Having become bored of trying to sleep and failing, he jumped into the shower. As the hot water poured on to his body, he felt calmer and his tense muscles started to relax. The hot water always eased his aching arm; the relief from the pain was always welcome. He wished he could stand for hours just enjoying the hot water flowing over him relaxing and cleansing his body. He was now feeling more revitalised and awake, lifting his head upwards to feel the water on his face. As he closed his eyes, a face began to form in his mind. It was slightly blurred but he could make out the fine features of a young woman's face, delicate but strong features, revealing a beauty he had never seen before, but then in a flash it was gone. It was the girl in his thoughts. He opened his eyes, the water still pouring over his face …

Torri woke up with a start. The dream had been very vivid, the man's face was so clear, she could almost touch it. His short dark hair framed his strong jaw line and complimented his large dark brown eyes. He was running towards her, shouting her name but as he was about to touch her she woke. This, she remembered, was the face she had seen before, when she had felt the pain in her arm. She felt she should know him but still could not recall him. Her gift had taught her long ago, that nothing happened by chance and things were sent to her for a reason. Not that things were always clear straight away but would become clear when the time was right. She closed her eyes again in a last effort to get some sleep, but try as she might, sleep would not come. Restless yet strangely excited, she got out of bed and decided to go to the one place that always gave her comfort and calmed her in times of stress or worry. Throwing on her jogging bottoms and a light sweater, she left her small clean home and headed towards the Nile. Just a ten minute walk, the fresh early morning air felt so good on her hot flushed cheeks. She needed to clear her head and there was something about the atmosphere at her favourite place which always instilled calmness in her so that she could relax or think clearly if she needed to. Why she felt such turmoil, she wasn't sure, just a feeling that came from deep within her being, oddly familiar but she just couldn't place it. At last she arrived and as she knelt down she immediately felt the calmness wash over her and she started to feel more relaxed. She gazed over the waters of the Nile, never ceasing to appreciate its beauty. Sunrise was still a few hours away but it was eerily quiet, almost too quiet and she realised that she had not even heard the usual tooting of the local owl that she had fondly called Olly. It was rare these days to have any local birds or wildlife so she had been overjoyed to discover Olly's existence. Every time she came here to find some peace, he always seemed to be there in the distance, giving out the occasional hoot almost as if he was reassuring her that he was there. Of course she had no idea if Olly was male or female but she always referred to him in the masculine. Sometimes she even found herself talking to him, laughing at herself silently to think that he could understand her, but he had become a friend and they seemed to share in the serenity of this special place. She was suddenly distracted from her thoughts about Olly as her eyes were drawn to the water, the moonlight was casting a silvery light on the gentle ripples and as she gazed at the light, it seemed to grow brighter until it looked almost like a circle of light hovering on the water's surface. She had become mesmerised looking at the light, her thoughts wandering to the old beliefs of lights being that of Astral Messengers. She was smiling at these thoughts, thinking it was just a trick of the moon but it didn't seem to be going away so she slowly stood up to look closer. It was now a definite circle completely filled with light but not too bright to hurt her eyes. It held her transfixed; she couldn't seem to look away and her heart began to race. The circle of light appeared to come closer to her, slowly at first and then in a burst of energy. The circle of light was over her in a flash. It was too quick for her to move and completely covered her, the light was so bright. A surge of heat consumed her body and as quickly as it had come, it disappeared; she felt the release from its grip. Feeling drained and faint, she fell to her knees, quickly putting out her hands in front of her to stop herself from falling on her face. After a few minutes she began to feel a little steadier so she slowly put her hands out in front of her. They were trembling, she felt so weak. Her left wrist felt hot and as she looked down she saw that around her wrist was the most exquisite bracelet. It appeared to be made of solid gold although it wasn't heavy. It had one single charm hanging from it. There was no clasp, it was a perfect fit, not tight but flush to her wrist so that it would not go over her hand as she tried to remove it. The single charm glistened in the moonlight. It was circular in shape with a gold edge but the centre of it seemed to be transparent with a faint violet hue. It felt warm to the touch and as she frantically tried to remove the bracelet, it got warmer and warmer until it began to feel uncomfortable. When she stopped trying to get it off, it began to drop in temperature and felt more comfortable. She sat back down, her heart pounding in the aftermath of this strange experience. She had to try and make some sense of this. She was, after all, used to experiencing unusual events of a spiritual nature but this was not her usual vision, it had been a real physical event with the bracelet as solid proof that it had happened, as if she could ever doubt it. What was this bracelet for and why had she got it? Questions, questions, but no answers. She took a closer look at it. Golden and bright but on closer inspection she could just make out some strange symbols within the violet hue of the charm. They were hardly noticeable at first but she found that as she stared at the charm they appeared to glow one by one, appearing in a sequence; each one coming to the front becoming larger before the next symbol started to appear. They seemed to pulse with the violet hue, almost like a heartbeat. What did they mean? An ancient language, signs of something, a warning, a message? What? What? What? …

She knew she had to find out, this after all was probably why she had been chosen to wear it and she had no doubt that she had been chosen. Perhaps she knew someone who could help her. That was the feeling she was consumed with as she quickly got up to return home; any thoughts of trying to remove it, strangely gone …

Chapter Seven

Patrick's car horn broke the early morning tranquillity, as he pulled up outside Joshua's small two up two down cell. This was the new name for all living accommodations which were all ultimately provided by T.R.I.G.O.M. Everyone had the opportunity of requesting personal preference for their décor if required to make them seem more individual but most people were happy as long as their Avatar worlds were in place and functioning. The horn was Patrick's own addition to his vehicle which he acquired from his old grandfather's treasure chest of times past. Horns were something which were not used or needed in this modern world and looked upon with distaste and disgust by anyone unfortunate enough to be on the receiving end of it. Patrick had never been one for patience and didn't like to be kept waiting. Josh rushed outside, with his bag flung over his shoulder, running out so that Patrick would not feel the need to sound his horn again. It was only just 8.30 on a warm Sunday morning and his neighbours would certainly not appreciate an early morning wake up call. He had found it hard to fit in when he had first moved into the district. His neighbours had looked upon him suspiciously at first. A young man of 27, what trouble would he bring? It was pretty obvious what they had thought initially but over time they had come to like this cheerful but studious young man. He always tried to be polite and helpful, not succumbing to late night activities or loud music, but enjoyed his studies and worked hard. He was now accepted and so certainly didn't want to upset them in any way.

"Shhhhh," Josh whispered to Patrick as he hurriedly ran towards the car but he was smiling, it was good to see his old friend. The excitement of a new adventure and all the questions he wanted to know of their task swirled round his head.

They spent the next hour with general catch up and news of trivialities that had happened in their lives. Patrick was genuinely concerned about Josh's wellbeing after the accident and asked him about the events of that night. "They never traced the car that night," Josh said as he was summarising events of his accident, wincing slightly at the painful memories.

"That's odd, me old friend, woulda thought with the cameras and computer controlled systems and all that rubbish, it should never have happened and at least would have been on the monitors."

"Mmmm," Josh uttered thoughtfully. That too was what he had been thinking and he had been unable to the get to the bottom of it and it troubled him more than he was letting on.

Patrick saw his troubled look. "Ah well, modern technology is not everything it's cracked up to be," he jokingly responded, trying to make light of it and hopefully change the subject to dissipate the frown that had clouded Josh's face. Josh decided to jump straight in with questions of where they were heading and why. It was Patrick who was now frowning and he looked troubled when Joshua asked about the commission. Patrick told him he would explain later but he was happy to tell him the place they were going to in Egypt. Josh thought this was a little strange but decided to leave it for the time being, knowing that Patrick must have his reasons and so he was happy to listen to Patrick as he explained. They were heading towards a little town called Atbara, situated right by the eastern side of the Nile.

Josh knew of Atbara, he had covered its history in one of his learning sessions. Many decades ago, this town was well known throughout the Sudan and where the British had won their Sudanese battle way back in 1898. It had also played a big part in the quest for peace in the Middle East. A town rich in water from the Ethiopian mountains and had a flourishing population. It had now been 15 years since peace in the Middle East had been celebrated and with a computerised road system, in line with all the cities of the world, it was a far cry from the old days of poverty and crime. Advancement in the understanding of human genes and DNA structures had also been put to use in changing behaviour, something which had caused controversy when it had first been implemented. Still, amongst certain groups, usually of the older generations, strong concerns still remained of this 'help' for advancement in the human evolution and the dependency on the computer. T.R.I.G.O.M. controlled all vital parts of the world's cities, which included all travel networks. The old world wide web of the past had been consumed long ago by new reforms and so now there was nothing else but T.R.I.G.O.M.

T.R.I.G.O.M. had been born out of great adversity, when monetary problems and natural climate change had re-sculptured the planet and living habits beyond recognition, posing great challenges for the human population to overcome if they were to survive and adapt. A worldwide crisis, never recorded by mankind before had brought all the great nations together, a feat that in itself would have never have been thought possible centuries ago. As in the past, out of a great disaster, war and adversity, came positives that could never have been before and this change bonded people together of all nations and cultures. They had begun to work for a common cause, helping each other rather than working against each other. Working together had been the only way forward for any chance of survival. To achieve this, technology took great leaps forward, cultures gradually changed and from panic and desperation, a new order was formed. Although peace was established, many of the older generation believed it came with a price. Relinquished freedom and the human essence of exploration and interaction with nature had been changed, instead people now relied on the protocols written by the newly formed council. T.R.I.G.O.M. was now the controller of all things and a brand new culture had been created.

Patrick's vehicle although fully integrated into T.R.I.G.O.M., was his sole use vehicle, something which was not common but still allowed. Most people only summoning transport as and when they were needed which were provided from the main core of

T.R.I.G.O.M. vehicles. He had inputted all the co-ordinates and sat back for the journey ahead. This meant that T.R.I.G.O.M. had complete control of the vehicle and would use the superhighways to get them to their destination and then transport them to their Air Disc. The Air Discs had long since taken over from the old conventional form of flight. It used a revolutionary power source of anti-gravitational force and allowed passengers to stay within their own vehicles if they so wished. Less contact with other passengers meant that the risks of viral and bacterial infections were now no longer a problem and the pollution of the old forms of air travel was no more. The discs themselves were deceptively large inside and had vast maneuverability with speeds beyond the sound barrier. If someone from the distant past were to have observed one, they would have thought that aliens with flying saucers had indeed invaded the planet as foretold in many a science fiction novel.

The nearest Air Disc Station, A.D.S. for short, was only an hour away and so Patrick looked over at his friend of many years and thought how tired and troubled he looked. Josh was rubbing his arm which had been broken in the crash. "Giving you some jip, pal?" Patrick enquired.

"Yeah, it just aches now and again since the accident but think I might have to go and get it checked out. Just got this sore bit which seems to be getting worse, it almost looks like a tattoo," he jokingly replied.

"Best get that looked at then, we don't want it dropping off." Patrick was laughing as he spoke. Josh also laughed at this but he couldn't help feeling a little worried that perhaps his arm was not healing as it should have …

Chapter Eight

The hour had passed so quickly and now the A.D.S. was ahead. No long queues, unlike the old days of motorway travel, road works and airport passenger controls. All travel was co-coordinated by T.R.I.G.O.M. which meant that no one had to wait. The vehicle moved smoothly up to the entrance point, I.D.s and personal data for authorised travel were electronically transferred within a split second, allowing them to move through the A.D.S. entrance zone without having to stop. Josh glanced over to his left and saw the Red Zone. Hardly used now, it was the place that the computer transferred any "unauthorised" travellers. It seemed to have a dark light emanating from it which actually made Josh shiver as they passed. As T.R.I.G.O.M. gained more control, it would be hard to travel anywhere without authorisation. People were now less inclined to do physical activities. Walking and exercise was discouraged whilst dependency on T.R.I.G.O.M. for every need was encouraged more and more. Obesity, which had grown to almost epidemic levels in the early 2000s had been controlled by re-programming human DNA to control fat levels, however, bone structures and energy levels were weaker through lack of exercise. Anyone wanting to keep fit and build up muscle had to do so privately, almost secretly.

Their vehicle moved swiftly to the waiting Air Disc Pad; its doors open ready to receive them. The automated voice of T.R.I.G.O.M. spoke, telling them that they were entering the Disc Zone and they would not be allowed to move from their vehicle until after takeoff. It was a soft relaxing voice but still Josh found its metallic tone cold and emotionless which always unsettled him. Being one for the outdoors he did not like the control that T.R.I.G.O.M. had over so many vital functions. In his innermost thoughts was that the computer wanted a weaker human race with complete dependency on T.R.I.G.O.M. He knew that many stories had been written about rogue computers and robots wanting to take over the world. The age old book of Arthur C Clarke's 2010 came to mind, one of the many books which he had read as part of his historic studies. He knew that T.R.I.G.O.M. was only working to protocols written by the "Scientific Board" but he couldn't help feeling uncomfortable with it.

Josh looked upwards and could see many Air Discs taking off, hovering for a few seconds before they sped upwards and vanished at great velocity towards their destination. Josh and Patrick headed towards their designated Air Disc. It was silver in colour and their vehicle docked inside with ease. A green hue surrounded them as the disc doors closed. T.R.I.G.O.M. confirmed their destination and they heard a low humming noise as the gravitation field was initiated. Their car was securely fixed into the docking gel which was a substance combined of organic and synthesized matter, linked to the main frame computer and was able to surround any type of vehicle and ensure that it was secure for the journey. The disc lifted off the ground as the force field built up to the appropriate levels for the journey. Within a few seconds they were speeding towards the hemisphere to reach their allotted flight path for their journey to Egypt. The journey would take an hour at the current speed they had been allotted, so they had a little time to enjoy the comforts provided on the Air Disc. They were able to leave their vehicle and walk around, completely stable due to the gravitation field which surrounded them. They headed towards the viewing platform, where they could look down on the Earth in its splendour and enjoy a beverage of their choice. It truly was an amazing experience looking out through the bubble window. The disc itself was able to fly vertically or horizontally, changing its position as required to conform with air flows and allocated air space, but all cargo and passengers remained in their own bubble of gravitation in their normal upright position and able to walk around with ease. Even though the disc was flying at tremendous speed, the flight was smooth and only the low humming of the computer could be heard. Music was available if requested and all things were provided by the onboard computer which instantly recognised voice commands.

Sitting stations were scattered around so that they could sit and enjoy the views, enjoy a beverage, listen to music or, as proved most popular, escape into an ever expanding virtual world. Josh and Patrick were both alike on this matter, they certainly had no time for a "virtual world escape" but both chose to sit quietly and ponder on their own thoughts.

Chapter Nine

Josh looked over at his friend who was sitting looking out of the window. He looked troubled and Josh sensed that perhaps all was not how it seemed. After all he was being very mysterious about the whole project and hadn't really told him anything substantial, but he had decided not to pressure him but rather to let him tell him in his own time. After all, he trusted him and felt sure that there were reasons he had not explained everything. He loved his old friend and they had been such close friends at school. They had both been lucky enough to attend the physical classes rather than virtual classes run by T.R.I.G.O.M. The classes had been small, as even then, their popularity was dwindling, parents and children preferring not to mix and stay within their own confinements. On his first day, Patrick had entered the classroom with such gusto and excitement, wanting to meet new friends and in his excitement he had tripped over his rather large feet and ended up in a heap on the floor in front of Josh. Josh had burst out laughing, but had held out his hand and helped him up. Patrick had thankfully seen the funny side too and they had both laughed. This proved to be typical of Patrick, feet first then thinking after but they had become firm friends and almost inseparable. Josh had sometimes wondered why they had become good friends, they were so different. Patrick was more extravert in his ways and was easily distracted from his work, particularly if a pretty girl was involved. Josh however was more reserved, although he could charm when he wanted to but he was quieter and preferred to study, easily losing himself in his work or an old book. However, their differences never seemed to matter, they had a strong friendship, their differences made their bond of friendship stronger. They were there for each other, no matter what, such was their friendship and their shared loved for knowledge of the past and future.

Patrick had been staring into space, wondering where all the time had gone since he had last seen his friend and where this project was going to ultimately take them. Since they had both graduated, they had always remained in touch but the times in between had got longer and longer, although this never mattered, they always picked up where they had left off and it was always as if they had only seen each other the day before. He hadn't told Josh too much about how he had been given this project, he had his reasons. Egypt was getting closer, he had been there once before, many years ago as a child when his parents had to stay for a couple of months, something to do with his father's work. He had always loved the place, it held a soft spot in his heart which had inspired him to take the career choice he did. He started to reflect; most of his time there had been happy but he had developed a boyish crush on one of the local girls. Little Megan he had called her and he starting putting in all his efforts to woo her. For a time they had shared young love but after a while she changed, becoming distant and quiet. He thought it had become one sided, not having the maturity of years to ask what the problem was and so his pride had taken a battering when she had eventually told him she didn't want anything more to do with him and much preferred the company of her old school friend. He had been deeply hurt and part of him felt that she did still want him and hadn't really meant the cruel words that had broken his heart. He had tried to woo her back but she had ignored his advances and pleas to see him again but had eagerly taken all the little tokens of his love that he had bestowed on her giving him a little hope that he would see her again one day. One of these gifts that he had given Megan was his precious 2030 memorabilia almanac given to him by his grandfather. She had just taken it and walked away without saying a word to him, just giving him a half smile and he couldn't make out if she was perhaps hiding something from him. That strong feeling that she too, didn't want to end their relationship. After this he had been so upset that he had to run off to hide the tears of embarrassment and hurt which he had felt. He ran and ran not knowing where he was going, until, exhausted, he stopped and sat down to catch his breath. He had started to sob like he had never done before but now after a few minutes he was smiling as he remembered fondly those innocent boyhood memories, that gentle touch of a woman's hand on his shoulder, as she lifted up his head. She was an elderly lady who possessed such beauty and had such love in her eyes, he instantly felt better and calmed. She merely stroked his cheek and placed something in his hand, kissing his head before walking away. He had put it down to his over active imagination, but it was like she had just dissolved and vanished before his eyes. He never knew who she was and he had never seen her again. In his hand he had discovered a little gold trinket. He didn't know what it was, it looked like a letter made of gold, but he had always kept it and referred to it as his good luck charm. He now wore it around his neck; he never went anywhere without it. He was inadvertently stroking the charm around his neck as he was remembering and Josh made him jump as he prodded him. "You fallen asleep there? You're not much company, come on, we're nearly there."

After exactly one hour, as they had been informed by T.R.I.G.O.M., they were instructed to return to their vehicle after which the disc took a quick descent and hovered briefly over the landing pad, then, very smoothly; it made a perfect landing, within the docking circle they had been allocated.

The doors of the disc opened and T.R.I.G.O.M. continued to take control of their vehicle for the rest of their journey. At last they had arrived in Egypt and were on their way to Atbara and heading towards a small short stay accommodation that Patrick had booked. There were still a few of these scattered about but were becoming a rarity and seldom used.

Josh decided to ask Patrick more about this commission, which he had seemed a little reluctant to discuss on their journey. He started to ask but again Patrick was reluctant to discuss it and told

Josh he would talk to him about it when they reached their accommodation. He signalled towards the on board computer, as if he didn't want to be overheard and quickly changed the subject. Josh realised that Patrick didn't want T.R.I.G.O.M. to hear and Josh nodded to show that he understood. They travelled the rest of the journey in silence, just looking out at the scenery and taking in the wonder of the place, so full of history and mystery, yet due to modern technology the roads and highways were just like any other part of the world. Each country had started to lose most of its uniqueness and seemed to have become as one. The main stays however, like the great pyramids, remained, as did other major monuments throughout the world. High tech buildings surrounding and overpowering them, but they were still there for those who would look to find them. The words of his professor coming to mind again. "These artefacts bring us knowledge to embrace and hold the key to understanding our past but what of our future …?"

Chapter Ten

Torri ran all the way home after her strange experience, her heart pounding and her head swimming. She ran straight past the 24 hour coffee booth, which she had never done before. She couldn't usually resist the smell of freshly made coffee, but she did not stop until her door was in sight. As she put her hands to the door, which instantly recognised her and started to open, she caught sight of the bracelet on her wrist. Was it her imagination or did it seem to be glowing? She quickly stepped inside and the door closed behind her. The sun was now peaking over the top of the distant mountains, the sunlight gradually entering her small living quarters through the large bay shaped window. This had been one of her preferences to individualise her cell. Its position was one of the main reasons why she had requested this place as it was always in the light and had the most amazing views of the mountains. Although the back of her home led on to the street, the front, where her living room was situated, looked out on to the wilderness. Torri was not one for hustle and bustle, modern gadgets and all those high tech toys; she much preferred the old ways and things of natural beauty. She had felt lucky to have found this place and had begged the council to let her have it. No one owned their homes, which were called cells but were allotted them by the T.R.I.G.O.M. Council, however she worked hard for the council, showing potential and so they had granted her request. It was situated just on the outskirts of Atbara Town, within walking distance to the eastern side of the Nile but not too far from the city where she worked. Soft lighting came on automatically as she entered the living room, the computer gauging that the sunlight was not yet to its full capacity and some light was still required. Torri however did not require any generated light and so instantly requested "lights off". Her voice activated command immediately recognised and the lights went off. She sat down on her sofa, which was able to mould to her shape to give her maximum comfort and support. She needed a moment to relax and think about the events which had just taken place, even though she desperately wanted to shower and go to the coffee booth. She felt tired and lacked energy; she decided to just sit with the intention of resting her eyes a moment to see if she could make any sense of things. As she sat back she started to relax a little and her eyes began to close. She now felt like she was floating, almost weightless as she appeared to be drifting upwards. There was no fear or panic, just a calm and soothing feeling slowly engulfing her. Almost like a whisper, she heard, what she could only describe as a voice like soft tinkering bells. The words not clear to her ears but vivid in her thoughts so she understood even though she could not actually hear them. "The bracelet is a gift for you to protect and keep safe. All will become clear when the time is right. The road you are on has meaning, end and beginnings for future life, hold on to your faith and follow the signs."

She felt no fear just a sense of happiness as she seemed to be submerged in a violet light. No questions came to her mind, unusual for Torri who had such an enquiring mind, she just seemed to trust in what she was feeling. She must have fallen into a deep sleep after this as the next thing she knew she woke up with a start and looked up her digital time piece. It was now ten-thirty on a cloudy Sunday morning and she needed to move. The comforting words were still in her head but she was late and had no more time to think about it. The bracelet remained on her wrist, a constant reminder that it had not been a dream and had actually happened.

Torri worked in the main Scientific Research Building in down town Atbara. Her work consisted of gathering samples of earth and vegetation for analysis by T.R.I.G.O.M., which linked information from all over the planet for combined research and monitoring of any planetary changes. Even though outdoor activities were not encouraged, some physical work still had to be done and Torri loved being in the outdoors and would spend as much time as possible collecting her samples. There were no Monday to Friday, 9 until 5 jobs anymore, or very few existed, so even though it was Sunday, Torri had to work. She quickly showered, the hot water making her feel a little better, but she still felt tired. She couldn't take off the bracelet to shower but watched as the water seemed to flow over it without wetting it at all, for a moment it held her spellbound as if it had its own force field. Tired of thinking, she dried herself and put on suitable clothing for the day's task. She was picking up mud samples from one of the newly formed hot springs, close to her favourite spot near the Nile. She had also been given an assignment to travel to the great pyramids of Giza to take a sample of its increasingly decaying stone. She was looking forward to this immensely but that was tomorrow's project. For today she was quite happy pottering near home and perhaps it would help suppress these mixed feelings of excitement and foreboding. Torri set off, completely kitted out with vacuumed sample vessels, ready to transport back to T.R.I.G.O.M. once the required samples had been acquired. As the site was only a short distance from her home she had decided to walk and was glad of the cool air on her face as she headed to the hot spring.

Chapter Eleven

Atbara was in sight. Just before they reached the hotel Patrick leant over to his baggage and picked up a small case. He then put his hand on the metal dash and a small drop down compartment opened and he put the case inside and it closed. He looked at Josh and winked. Don't want my entire luggage scanned. The metal dash had closed flush and you would never have known that anything was there. "A slight addition added by my most talented self." He laughed patting the dash as he spoke but Josh wondered what it was that he did not want scanning by T.R.I.G.O.M. He had no time to enquire as at last they arrived and their vehicle pulled up outside the small but modern looking accommodation facility. The digital information was immediately sent to the in-house computer and its doors opened to welcome Patrick and Joshua. An automated luggage trolley emerged to scan and take their belongings. They didn't have to exert themselves in any way and the moving walkway assisted them into the reception area, where they were transferred on to a red moving strip which took them straight to their rooms. Manual walkways were available but were hardly used within this modern society. The car had been transferred to the parking area where it would remain until it was needed and new co-ordinates given to the onboard computer. Because the accommodation facility was fully computerised, few staff were required which did not sit well with Joshua, he liked the personal touch and enjoyed human contact. All the rooms appeared to be the same; small but bright, accommodating a bed, a wet room, a computer room and a small eating area. Food and drink were available, by a simple touch screen, showing available options of beverages and food. As requested, the items required would be transported into the room via the food and drink chamber which every room had, situated in the eating area. Public eating areas were seldom used these days and so few were provided, people preferring solitary habits. Direct personal contact was discouraged, although not forbidden; Josh was one of the few exceptions. He had started to feel peckish so looked at the food selection list; he was sure that Patrick would be doing the same in his room. They had arranged to meet in an hour, after settling in, unpacking and grabbing a bite to eat. Now what did he fancy that was on the menu? Nothing appealed to him and he thought he would go out and see what else was available. He had noticed a coffee booth on the way to the hotel so decided he would try one and have some human contact rather than sit alone in his rather impersonal room. He walked towards the door and as his DNA recognition had been transferred to operate within the room, the door opened as he asked. Until his stay ended, the room could only be activated by himself, the hotel management or by the computer if it felt that any protocols had been broken or for any emergency situations. He didn't bother with the red moving strip, which was ready outside his door to take him to the lobby, but instead opted for the back staircase which looked like it hadn't been used for some time. He considered calling for Patrick but decided against it; he thought he would do a little exploring on his own first. Outside the hotel, the air was cool and it looked like rain was coming in. He slipped on his light jacket and pulled it together, this was a new idea in fastenings; put together, it automatically bonded together and then with a slight pull it would open again as required. He turned left as he remembered they had passed the coffee booth on their journey to the hotel. If he was right, it was only a couple of hundred yards down the road just around the sharp bend. As he turned the corner, he was correct, the coffee booth was just on the left. He could smell the aroma of fresh coffee which put a spring into his step. Some coffee booths were not manned at all and were completely automatic, serviced efficiently by T.R.I.G.O.M. A few of the old ones still remained however, offering a more personal service. Thankfully, for Josh, this was a manned coffee booth and as he stepped inside, he was amazed how big it actually was. There were tables and chairs, then it opened out into a dining area, taking on the old fashioned American Diner theme, which was very rare to find. He hadn't known that anything like this existed, it was like stepping back in time; it was like a jewel in the desert. No vehicles were parked outside, indicating that the place would be empty as no one walked anywhere, apart from the odd exception. Josh was proud to be different. Indeed it was empty and he couldn't help but smile as he looked around, pleased at finding such a treasure. A small woman, who looked about 50, stood behind the counter. It was so nice to see someone with a welcoming face that clearly had not had the fashionable replacement facial graft. Most people did not look any older than 30 or an age of their choice, due to advancements in cosmetic and DNA surgery. A small piece of skin could be used to form a flawless cover of the original face and features of the person it had been taken from so that anytime a line or wrinkle appeared, the facial skin could be replaced as simply as putting on a hat or a scarf or for minor work, it could be modified at one of the specially modified computer terminal interfaces.

As he approached the small counter, she smiled at him and beckoned him closer. "Well, young man, I am Evia and what can I get for you?" There were also rows and rows of old fashioned cookies and cakes, the like he had only ever seen in books. He was amazed at the choice of foods as well as coffee and tea. He had his usual strong black coffee but couldn't resist a rather large chocolate chip cookie. He decided to sit close to the counter so that he could look out through the large windows and also chat to Evia. The coffee was the best he could ever remember tasting, strong but not bitter and he immediately felt relaxed as he took a bite of his cookie. Evia was a kindly lady and explained she had lived in Atbara for 80 years. Josh was astonished, she certainly had a few lines and wrinkles but seemed so sprightly and agile that he would have only placed her at being around the 50 mark. She was highly delighted when he passed on this observation and promptly topped up his coffee. He enquired about the locals and places of interest, to which she was more than happy to relate tales of local history and historical sites. As she started to mention a cave that was nearby, called the Cave of Symbols, his interest heightened but just then, like a whirlwind, a girl rushed into the booth and Evia smiled.

"Late for work again, Torri? Here's your coffee and I have put it in a bag with one of my special cakes."

"Oh, Evia, you are a life saver." She giggled. "Need to see you later, I need your advice," she said as she grabbed the bag, and then as she spun round her eyes met Josh's. For a split second, time seemed to stand still and they both stared at each other with an instant recognition and a feeling of being found. In a flash this special moment was gone; she was running late, she couldn't stop and only managed to smile at him as she dashed for the door. Josh got up, but she had disappeared out of the door. He could still see her running down the road and then she was out of sight as she rounded the corner.

Evia laughed. "That's our Torri; lovely girl and never misses her coffee but often running late and always in a rush."

Josh sat still for a moment, unable to speak just looking out of the window, hoping that she would appear again but she didn't. That was the face that he had seen, he was sure of it and he had to find out more about her. He tried to casually ask Evia more about her, but he could sense that she intuitively knew that he was more than just casually interested. Evia described her as friendly, loved her work with a passion but didn't seem to have too many friends, which she assumed was because she was always working or maybe because she processed special gifts.

"Special gifts?" Josh enquired, but Evia just smiled and replied, "We all have specials gifts of one sort or another." She looked at him intently as she spoke. It was almost as if she had spoken to his soul. He brushed aside a steadily growing uneasy feeling and decided perhaps it would be best to change the subject.

He reminded her about the "Cave of Symbols" and after a short pause she continued. "It's a short distance from here just over the hill top there." She pointed straight ahead and he looked to see a large hill in the distance, surrounded by cloud but didn't appear to be too far away. "On one side of the wall are ancient drawings of symbols which have never been deciphered," she continued. "Some have speculated that they are messages from a previous civilisation or even from visitors to our planet." She looked around nervously as she spoke. "There are those who would not allow us to talk of such things and so you must be careful of whom you ask questions." She then promptly picked up his empty coffee cup and asked him if he would like some more. Even though he would have loved another cup and to learn more about the caves, he politely refused, realising it was time he went back to the hotel to meet back up with Patrick. He was intrigued about these caves but also a little concerned about the seeming secrecy that had been inferred. Why had he never heard of them before in all his learning and expeditions? A mystery that had intrigued him. Without further questions, he gave her a big smile and told her he would see her later. No money transactions were ever conducted now as each person had an I.D. chip implanted at birth. The computer would have scanned him as he entered the booth and deducted credits from his allotted amount. A small star-like scar on the left hand of each person was the only indication that the chip was present. This was left in case the implant needed to be changed or upgraded at any time. The chip also recorded activities of its owner and any information which T.R.I.G.O.M. may require and which could be retrieved at any time. Anyone who tried to alter a chip or have it taken out, would be quickly dealt with. Not many people were around to relate what happened under these circumstances. Josh took Evia's hand to give her a cheeky kiss goodbye and she laughed as he walked out of the booth. As he headed back to the hotel he suddenly realised that Evia's hand had been smooth and unless he had been mistaken, she had no scar on her left hand …

Chapter Twelve

As he rounded the corner the hotel was in sight and Patrick was waiting outside looking around nervously. Josh walked briskly up to him smiling, but Patrick didn't return the smile. "Where have you been?" he asked worriedly, touching his good luck charm around his neck, almost as if he needed reassurance. Josh explained that he had just fancied looking around and had found a nice coffee booth just around the corner, he couldn't understand why Patrick appeared so nervous. "Well that sounds good to me, fancy another?" Patrick said.

"Yeah, why not? You OK, mate, you seem a little agitated?" Josh asked him concerned.

Patrick just shrugged and said he wanted to discuss their project in a quieter place so they could go over their plans and had merely wondered where he had gone. Josh thought this a little strange but he was still full of thoughts of that mysterious girl and the "Cave of Symbols" which Evia had told him about. For some reason he didn't feel inclined to tell Patrick about the girl and thought he would save it for another time, although he didn't understand why he should feel like that. After all Patrick was a good and trusted friend.

They set off and within a few minutes arrived at the coffee booth. As they stepped inside, Josh looked eagerly around for Evia so that he could introduce her to Patrick but he could not see her anywhere. Strangely there were no cookies on the bar and the machines looked like they were just set for self-service. He was puzzled as it had not been that long since he was here. He presumed that she had gone off duty or was taking a break somewhere and put it to the back of his mind. They both helped themselves to a large coffee for which the computer scanned their hands and sat down by the table near the window. Josh realised that when he had coffee before he had not been scanned and the booth seemed different but he put this fleeting thought to the back of his mind, he was now eager to learn of this "commission" that Patrick seemed to be so guarded about. He had become concerned about his friend's sudden change in mood and so placing his arm on his he asked Patrick to tell him of their commission and how it had come about …

Patrick drew in a long breath and started to explain … Two weeks ago, whilst on a short trip to visit his father's old friend in his ancestry village of Doolin, he had by chance bumped into an old man, which was a rare sight nowadays to see someone so old looking. He had gone into the local coffee booth which had been quite full and as there was a spare seat near Patrick, the old man had sat himself down opposite and started to pass the time of day. For someone to want to converse was very unusual these days and Patrick, one for conversation, was intrigued by this elderly gentleman and enjoyed the chance to chat. Either by clever navigation or chance, the conversation got on to the state of the world's climate and then progressed to ancient artefacts, the old man showing particular interest in the golden charm around Patrick's neck. He had told the old man that he had been given it many years ago and then went on to tell him of his own interest in ancient artefacts and the papers he had written on their relevance to the future. The chance meeting had concluded with the old man, who by then had introduced himself as Admar, asking Patrick to meet him at his office with the possibility of work in that field. Patrick had tried to ask him what that may entail but Admar had said that they would discuss it at his office and proceeded to write down the address on a piece of paper using an old type pen. This was quite odd, as all things now were usually sent via computer, or digital equipment. Pens, pencils and paper were old antiques. Admar then suggested that as his place was not too far away, that perhaps Patrick could walk; again, another strange request. They set up a date for the following evening at 1800 hours and Admar gave him the piece of old paper with the address written on it. Patrick had not taken much notice of what he was writing down but when he had gone, Patrick looked at the address that the old man had written down. It was written beautifully in an old ink pen, with flowing artistic strokes which said *The Doolin Caves, left by the stalactite, I will be waiting.* Patrick was amused and only now considered that this may not have been a chance meeting and was probably some kind of wind up by a slightly crazy old man. He was absolutely baffled by the address the old man had given him and even if it was just a joke his curiosity had got the better of him and there was no way he was going to miss this meeting even if it turned out to be a hoax. He gently stroked his golden charm, a habit he had when he was thinking or unsure of anything.

Chapter Thirteen

The Doolin caves had been a main attraction for the area many decades ago, the large stalactite still hung near the entrance of the cave, a truly beautiful phenomenon of nature which used to cause much wonder and interest. Sadly, the caves had now been virtually forgotten; the modern world, not interested in the Earth's natural wonders or things of a physical nature, where walking and exploring might be involved. The caves themselves were shielded with a natural ore that could not be penetrated by signals like radio waves and such like. It was not a place that T.R.I.G.O.M. required or could operate in, hence any interest in these kinds of places were greatly discouraged.

Patrick used to secretly visit the caves when he was a little boy and being similar to Josh in that regard, he was a natural explorer and the ways of this modern culture could not suppress his true nature. The few people that still felt urges to walk and explore were frowned upon by society and few had the chance to feed their natural instincts or if they did, it was quietly and discreetly. Patrolling probes were everywhere, making it difficult for anyone to go unnoticed and only those who had a genuine reason, were allowed to undertake physical activities to any great degree. However, the inclination to be less active was well ingrained in the human culture now so it did not cause too many problems or incidents for T.R.I.G.O.M.

Patrick pondered on which would be the best way to the caves without being too conspicuous or arousing any interest by T.R.I.G.O.M. He remembered that there was a small dirt path which still linked the caves with the village that went via the old cliffs of Moher. It was never used these days and was probably well overgrown with shrubbery. Luckily it was well into the winter months and it was starting to get dark well before the meeting was planned. He smiled to himself, it felt like a mysterious adventure. He didn't think that anything would come of it but, it was just a silly little boy's game of spies. He smiled at his boyish thoughts, secretly enjoying the intrigue. Oh to have been a boy in the mid 1900s. He had always been enthralled by the old books that his grandma had given him, which had been passed down through the family. He would read the old adventure books, late into the night, often with his light generator under the bed clothes so that he would not be detected by the computer, which was pre-set to report his activities after his sleep curfew. This had been programmed by his parents, but he had discovered that it did not seem to be able to detect his secret reading arrangements. He liked the fact that he could fool the computer; it was not infallible and for some reason this made him feel good.

Before he knew it, he found himself planning his journey to the old caves, under cover of the shrubbery and darkness. He wasn't too sure how long it would take so he decided that he would set off as soon as it started to get dark. As soon as darkness fell, Patrick set off dressed in some old dark clothing that he found, not made from the new fabric which he always thought had some sort of traceability by T.R.I.G.O.M. He was aware that his identification chip was always present but as long as he acted normally, the main street cameras and patrol drones would have no reason to stop him and once at the caves, no signals could be transmitted. He suddenly wondered why he was being so secretive. After all, he wasn't doing anything wrong, but he sensed strongly that this was the right course of action. Rain was falling again and it was cold, so he pulled up his collar on his coat and donned the old hat with the large brim, which belonged to his grandfather and which was brilliant for keeping the rain from his face. He didn't really know why he had kept the old hat but he was glad of it now and it reminded him of past times. He was more and more convinced that this was just a hoax but he was just enjoying the sense of adventure. It was how he imagined being child decades ago would have felt; he was acting a part of a great detective perhaps. The streets were deserted, no one walked very far and by this time they were usually submerged into their virtual lives, which people were now becoming more and more dependent on. T.R.I.G.O.M. vehicles breezed past him, the occupants too preoccupied to notice him, probably just wanting to get home to link up to their computerised world. At last he saw the side street which would lead him to the old path and he sighed with relief that it was still there and looked to be accessible. He quickly turned off the main street, noticing that one of the cameras was starting to turn his way. Luckily he managed to disappear on to the path before it turned fully. Once on the path, it felt like a different world and strangely quiet. At first he couldn't understand why it felt so different and then he realised, it was because he could not hear the humming of the computer systems overhead or underground. The silence was incredible, he had never realised the extent that T.R.I.G.O.M. had become integrated into human life and how dependency on it had grown. People did not seem to think for themselves, which Patrick believed to be the fundamental nature and reason for existence of human beings. Nature didn't seem to be important anymore, other than specially bred animals for eating and sustenance. Even these were reducing in numbers, as laboratory processed foods were being heavily promoted and natural foods less favoured by T.R.I.G.O.M.

It was obvious that no one had used this path for many years and it was very overgrown with trees and shrubbery, which made walking quite tricky and tiring. Although he did like the outdoors, he was after all still part of this modern society and did not exercise as much as he would have liked. After about half an hour, he had to take a break and catch his breath; he couldn't believe how unfit he actually was. He found a large rock and sat down to rest for a few minutes. He had the foresight to bring his light generator with him but did not shine it upwards just in case of detection from any overhead surveillance probes which were often sent out at night. He looked ahead to see where his path was taking him. He had started to ascend up over the cliffs and knew that the cave was at the top point, tucked away inside a little grove. He didn't want to sit around for too long and as soon as he had caught his breath, continued upwards on the cliff path. After what seemed like an eternity, he could see the rock face where he knew the cave would be. It had been a long time since Patrick had been to the cave and it seemed to be surrounded by some sort of plant which he didn't recognise. As he drew closer, he could see the mouth of the cave through the entanglement of leaves and branches. As he drew up to the cave entrance he realised that it was not blocked by any part of the surrounding woodland which indicated that it must have been used recently and on a regular basis. "Some office," he thought and smiled.

He took a quick glance at his time piece. He was about half an hour early so perhaps after a little rest he could have a look around before Admar was due to arrive. It never occurred to him that he could be in any danger, he just felt excited. Through the mouth of the cave, he thought he noticed a bench-like rock, ideal for resting and so without further thought he entered the cave. He was expecting to see the old stalactite hanging in the darkness, but as he walked further a blue light seemed to illuminate the cave so that he could actually clearly see his surroundings. The old stalactite was still there but appeared to be half the size he could remember as a young boy. It was completely surrounded in this strange blue light. He looked around for the bench-like stone that he had seen, which was indeed a bench actually carved out of the stone itself. He was sure that this had never been there all those years ago. Thankful for somewhere to sit, he sat down on the bench. As soon as he had sat down, the blue light began to glow brighter and the stalactite started to pulsate. The stone bench, which he had expected to be cold was instead very warm; suddenly, it too, started to pulsate. He could still see his surroundings but they seemed very blurred and started to fade away, fading in and out of his visions. Gradually other objects started to appear in their place until finally the cave and its surroundings had disappeared. Now, instead he was in a large grand old room, no longer sat on a stone bench but rather a golden chair, elaborately carved with a cushion of red velvet. The vibrations were now beginning to lessen so that his new surroundings became clearer and right before him stood the old man he had met in the coffee booth.

"Hello, Patrick." Admar smiled.

Chapter Fourteen

Patrick was a little disoriented which made him feel dizzy; he was unsure what had just happened. Admar shook his hand warmly and told him not to worry and that the dizziness would soon subside. "You are still in the same place, Patrick, but in a different vibration which has always existed, like a world within a world, to put it into simplistic terms."

Patrick looked dazed, not understanding a word that Admar had said. He went on to explain that at this point, Patrick should not try too much to understand and in time everything would make sense. Patrick thought he saw figures in the far distance, like distant shadows but with a faint glow but too far away to make out their real shapes. Admar distracted him as he offered him a drink of water and then when he looked again the shadows had vanished. Admar smiled at him and explained further.

"All matter is never lost, it changes into other forms and just like when a person dies on Earth, they are not lost just changed and live on but within a vibration that cannot be seen by those still in the physical form on Earth. Perhaps it would be best to describe it like a helicopter, an old type of air travel. The blades rotate slowly to start and you can quite clearly see all four blades, but as they speed up, you cannot see four separate blades, they look like one. Perhaps you could say the original version of virtual reality." He laughed out loud as he looked at Patrick. Patrick nodded, only half understanding what he said and still confused as to where he actually was and what he was doing there. Admar smiled at him trying to reassure him. "We should not dwell on how you got here but as to the reason why you are here.

"We have a very important job which we would like you to undertake. You have a friend called Josh, whom we would like you to recruit to assist you in your task should you choose to accept it."

"How did you know about my old friend Josh, when I have only just met you?" Patrick asked, feeling very odd and becoming increasingly uncomfortable.

Admar went on. "Please do not be alarmed, Patrick, but we have done our research. For such an important task we would not choose just anybody, as I am sure you would agree. For instance if you were interviewing a person for a position of importance, would you not make sure that the person has all the right qualities and contacts for the job? Besides, you were chosen a very long time ago." He looked at the charm around Patrick's neck but he didn't elaborate on that comment, instead he proceeded. "We have been the guardians of life symbols and other things which are older than you can ever imagine. This world of ours is due to evolve again, as it has done many times before, it is not to be looked upon as doom and gloom but more of a celebration for our advancement and learning, so it is to be embraced. This view, of course, would not be shared by the Scientific Council and the majority of the world's population, only because they have become self-obsessed with matters which are really not important and are losing their individuality. Dependence on the artificial intelligence has reached an unacceptable level, however, technology will play a part in our evolution." Admar looked at Patrick's face and smiled. "Try not to be too alarmed at what I am telling you, I know you can cope with it although you may not fully understand just yet. We need you to initiate a trip with Josh to the Great Pyramid of Giza. As you know, it is surrounded now, not by sand but by water due to the change in the world's climate over the last few decades. There is a particular area, which lies just below the water level, that is important. To an untrained eye, it looks like the many other stones which are part of the pyramid's structure but Josh, with all his experience in this field, will see that it is in fact, very different. It is important that you go quickly, as we know that the council may also be interested in this particular stone. They know it is important but not why, so it is vital that they do not discover its true purpose and so time is of the essence. It is something that we cannot undertake ourselves, but you, like your friend Josh, are well known for your interest and theories of ancient relics and monuments. Because of this it is less likely to create any unwarranted attention should you be stopped and questioned. The T.R.I.G.O.M. council seem to be more and more suspicious of anyone showing an interest in these sorts of areas but with you it would be quite plausible that you are there to gather samples in line with the work that you do. Events will take care of themselves but I can explain no further at this point."

He gave Patrick a large metal container for the pretence of taking samples should he be stopped which was made of an alloy metal that he did not recognise. His head was throbbing and although many questions were swimming around in his mind, he found himself too overwhelmed to speak. He just took the container along with the papers, which looked like old papyrus scrolls showing instructions of which area the stone needed to be approached from and where samples would be best obtained from. Admar explained that the purpose of these was to make their mission look like just a normal sample-taking excursion for their studies and which they could show to the T.R.I.G.O.M. council should they be stopped or questioned.

Patrick started to feel dizzy again and could only vaguely hear Admar's words as he continued to explain that many records had been destroyed by the Scientific Council in their misguided judgement that ancient symbols and writings were of no use and would only confuse, or even create unrest and panic in the modern world. Most of the writings could not be deciphered amongst the modern council of T.R.I.G.O.M. This did cause a problem for the council as they could not agree on a solution and were of divided opinions. Some theorised that they were written by other life forms before human kind walked the Earth; some believed them to be revelations of events which will come to pass, part of a cycle which has happened before, giving instruction on how the cycle would be completed, ensuring a life continuum. Because they did not understand, they destroyed many valuable artefacts. They considered it a sign of weakness on their part that they did not understand. However, some of the most important ancient writings and symbols had never been found by the council and had existed for many thousands of years, hidden away by the "old order" and guarded until the time for their intended purpose and only then would they be allowed to appear and be found.

After a moment Patrick regained some form of normality and asked, "The old order, who or what are they?"

At this point a woman stepped forward and kissed him warmly on both cheeks. "Hello, Patrick. My name is Evia and I am so very pleased to meet you again."

… Josh who had been sitting quietly listening to Patrick's tale gasped. Patrick drew his breath too as he was suddenly flooded with the memories of his childhood time in Egypt. It was the gentle face and tender touch of the woman who had placed his lucky charm in his hand all those years ago and which he had worn around his neck ever since. Josh gently whispered, "Evia …"

Chapter Fifteen

Torri had reached the hot springs in good time and started to collect samples. The air smelt of sulphur but was not too unpleasant. In no time she had her collection safely placed in her sample tubes, which were self-processing and mineral contents automatically processed and digitally sent to her laboratory computer. The rest of the substances would be kept safe in her temperature controlled case for further studies and analysis upon her return to work. Satisfied that her work here was finished, she allowed her mind to wander back to the young man in the coffee booth. She knew that this was the man in her visions, her heart had skipped a beat when their eyes had met but she was not worried that she had missed the chance of speaking to him. She trusted her belief that if they were meant to meet then it would happen, but even so, it had been a shock to see him in person, so close and in her place, as she lovingly referred to the coffee booth. This coffee booth had only been there a few months, replacing an old one which had been there for many years and had been in need of updating. She had been amazed that the old one had just seemed to have disappeared over night and the new updated one had stood welcoming her the next day. The old one had been completely automated but fronted with a typical T.R.I.G.O.M. advanced robotic intelligent machine that had been developed to supposedly add a more personal touch. This artificial life form had been nicknamed with combined affection and sarcasm by the locals as Alf. Alf was an old model and was prone to malfunctions often to the amusement and frustration of the locals. Great advancements had taken place since "Alf" had been created. Now Artificial Intelligence robots had been created with brain implants from organic sources which enhanced their human qualities. Their ability to calculate and function was far superior to humans but the emotional qualities were still evolving and far from matching their human counterparts. There was still a long way to go before they could even think about challenging the existence of human beings. Theories of the "machines rising" and exterminating all mankind, being the cause of many heated debates in the times when people could openly meet and voice their concerns. Now only the holographic meetings took place and these were closely monitored by T.R.I.G.O.M., with certain subjects completely forbidden.

Torri was not a great lover of Alf and any kind of robotic life form, so it was a relief to her that Alf disappeared with the old booth. Torri was over the moon when she discovered that this new booth had a real person in it; this was so rare, but she didn't question it she just embraced it. She had found a true friend in Evia, she knew as soon as she met her, that first day when she had walked in, greeted with one of Evia's special coffees and a large chocolate cookie. After that, Torri used the booth numerous times a day and Evia was always there, ready with her coffee, always had time for a chat and it soon seemed to Torri that she had known her all her life. She discovered that she could confide in her and so she found herself telling her all about herself and her "gift". Evia seemed to understand completely and she didn't treat her as if she was strange because of it, instead she took an interest in her and offered her advice and guidance. She always seemed to have wise words for her. Torri marvelled at how knowledgeable she was, her words always made sense and were spoken with such sincerity, that she was always calmed and felt at peace after their many conversations. She often thought that if her beloved grandfather had still been here, he too would have liked Evia; she reminded her so much of him. Torri never questioned the fact that Evia was always there, whatever time, whatever day, she just accepted it. Now, with the strange events of late, Torri wanted to complete her job quickly and then head to the coffee booth. She needed to talk to Evia, both about the man of her visions in the coffee booth and this strange bracelet that she had on her wrist. There was however somewhere she had thought of to go first.

Chapter Sixteen

After listening to Patrick's story, Josh sat in silence for a few minutes. He wasn't quite sure why he had made the connection through just hearing Evia's name but strange things seemed to be happening and he found himself telling Patrick about the friendly lady in the booth earlier whose name was also called Evia, not exactly a common name. Josh asked Patrick to describe her to him and his description matched perfectly. They both sat for a moment in silence, Josh trying to take in what Patrick had told him and Patrick still playing over his strange experience in his mind, trying to make sense of it. After a few minutes, which seemed to them both like hours, Josh asked, "What happened then?"

Patrick seemed a little vague, all he could remember was that he had taken the container and agreed to contact Josh. As soon as Evia had greeted him and he had felt her gentle kiss on his cheek, she seemed to fade and he found himself back on the bench in the cave. At first he wondered if it had all been a strange dream but he had the container and the instructions which Admar had placed in a small black case, gripped tightly in his hand. He sat for some time but as soon as he could muster up the strength, he returned home, retracing his steps back down the old path. He did not stop for a rest this time but carried on until he reached the safety of his own door.

Josh stared at Patrick; this day was getting stranger and stranger. Could this woman he described really be the same lady he had met earlier in the coffee booth? Who were these people and what was their purpose? The questions were too many to voice, instead Patrick and Josh could only stare at each other, completely silent. Josh broke the silence first but with so many questions buzzing around his head, he only managed to ask, "So when do we set off for Giza?"

Patrick hesitated for a moment and then suggested that they go at first light Monday and perhaps they should just enjoy the rest of the day and get themselves adjusted to the situation. Josh thought that this was a good idea, but although he needed to clear his head, he also needed to feed his curiosity and so he decided that he would take a walk over to the Cave of Symbols which Evia had told him about. This fresh air would do him good and at the same time he could investigate the cave. Patrick said that he was going back to the hotel to rest. Josh thought that he looked tired and perhaps that was a good idea, he needed some time to himself and had decided he would tell Patrick about the girl in his visions later over some dinner. They arranged to meet in the reception area at 7 p.m. and both went their separate ways but before they parted Patrick grabbed Josh and hugged him, something he did very rarely. "Take care, my friend," he said quietly.

Josh looked at him with concern. "Don't worry I will be seeing you shortly." Josh tried to reassure his friend but he too had a strange, anxious feeling which he was finding difficult to supress.

Chapter Seventeen

The air was cool when Josh got outside but at least it had stopped raining. He looked up at the sky, full of grey clouds with the odd glimmer of blue. His arm had begun to ache a little and he made a mental note that he must go back to the hospital and get it checked out as soon as he got back home. As he thought this, he touched his arm, his fingertips just gently rubbing his skin. It felt hard to the touch and a sudden shooting pain made him wince, but it soon passed. As he walked towards the cave, he started to reflect back to the night of his accident. He knew that he had been preoccupied but where did that vehicle come from so suddenly and why had there been no investigation into how it could have happened? All vehicles were controlled by T.R.I.G.O.M., everything monitored and yet when he had asked questions whilst he was recovering, he got no answers and everything was the usual "T.R.I.G.O.M. Classified". He realised that he was getting nowhere and had decided to have one last attempt to find out. He had just been about to file in another complaint when Patrick had contacted him. He harboured dark thoughts that T.R.I.G.O.M. might have been responsible; thoughts he hardly dared acknowledge but what reason would there be to try and harm him or yes, even kill him? He felt certain that his questions would never be answered.

He tried to steer his thoughts away from that night as he headed in the general direction of the caves, which Evia had told him about. Trying to concentrate on other things, anything else other than the accident, he decided that on the way back he would call again at the coffee booth to see if Evia was back on duty with the secret hope that he would bump into that girl again. His heart skipped a beat at this thought and he smiled to himself and felt much better.

He could now see what looked like the cave that Evia had described just a few hundred yards in front of him. So many thoughts had kept him so preoccupied that he had not realised quite how far he had walked. He smiled to himself as he realised that there were no T.R.I.G.O.M. drones or probes anywhere near the cave. He remembered what Patrick had told him, that caves had certain properties, which blocked out signals and all manner of air waves, making them places devoid of invasion from modern technology. "A breath of fresh air," he thought. He could now see the mouth of the cave and as he approached it, he felt in his coat pocket. Yes he had his light generator, something he mostly carried for his work; it was always a handy tool to have. With it firmly in his hand, he stepped inside the cave. Surprisingly it wasn't dark, there seemed to be a source of natural light, enough for him to see and not need the use of his light generator and so he slipped it back into his pocket. The cave felt warm inside and as he breathed in, he smelt an aroma, not unlike that of fresh soil. He remembered this smell, as a small boy he had watched his grandfather potting and growing his beloved plants. He would spend hours watching and chatting away, learning the obscure names of the various plants and always asking questions, which his grandfather took great pleasure in answering. Sadly, cultivating plants and any form of agriculture had become something of the past but his old grandfather had managed to keep an area in his home where he still grew some of the old varieties of house plants.

Now, the general human population lacked any interest and appreciation in this field. It was left to T.R.I.G.O.M. to manage and control plants and food needed to feed the populations; only the necessary plants had survived. Gardens for purely pleasure purposes, to admire the infusion of colour, smell and artistic design were long extinct and forgotten about. After his grandfather had passed away, it had left a great void in his life and now to smell fresh earth again brought back so many memories, bringing a smile to his face with the fond memories the smells conjured. With his thoughts still full of his childhood days, he casually walked further into the cave towards the far wall and then stopped suddenly. The wall was covered with strange symbols, the like he had never seen before. They were clear and precise, not faded at all which he would have expected for ancient drawings and writings. It looked like they had only just been painted. Some had vivid colour, which glowed as he stared at them and as he looked at the symbols his arm began to tingle. Just then he heard a rustle which made him jump. His tingling arm forgotten for a moment; he turned around startled as he heard footsteps behind him. As he turned, what he saw made him catch his breath and his heart almost stopped …

Chapter Eighteen

Torri smiled at him, she too was surprised to see him and they just stood for a moment both seemingly unable to move. It was Josh who moved first, he held out his hand and she gave him hers. "I think we already know each other," he whispered.

Her face glowed as she smiled back at him. "Yes, I believe we do."

Barely able to speak, she told him her name and that she had seen him in her dreams. She decided to say dreams rather than visions; she was unsure how he would react but she knew that he knew her too. He couldn't believe it and smiled as he told her that he had seen her face too in a dream and knew that they were meant to meet somehow, although he hadn't really understood how or why. Josh couldn't believe what he had just said, it sounded so cheesy and certainly not his usual style, but it was so true. He didn't feel embarrassed although he felt his cheeks burning as he looked at her but he knew instantly that she would understand. He felt an urge to kiss her but managed to steady himself. After all he had only just met her in person and he wasn't too sure of her reaction to him.

"What brings you to this cave?" she asked him.

He told her briefly about his background in ancient artefacts and his conversation with Evia at the coffee booth.

"Hmmm, Evia. Why does that not surprise me?" She laughed.

"I presume that you know her well then," Josh replied. Torri just smiled. "And what brings you to these caves, may I ask?" he continued.

Her smile faded a little, as if she was unsure of what to tell him or if she could trust him. It was only a momentary doubt, she knew that she could.

She found herself telling him about herself, her favourite place by the Nile and her job which entailed collecting samples which she enjoyed. She knew they were of a kindred spirit and that he would understand her love of the outdoors, her love of nature; not everyone she knew understood this passion of hers. She even found herself telling him about the strange ring of light which had engulfed her. He was so easy to talk to, she couldn't stop talking. Finally, after pausing for breath, she held up her hand so that he could see the gold bracelet, which was glowing brightly on her wrist. He took her hand gently to look at it, her hand was smooth to the touch and he wanted to pull her close. What was the matter with him? He had only just met this girl and he wanted to hold her so badly. He shook himself slightly and concentrated on the bracelet which was still glowing, its brightness intensifying as he stared at it, just as Torri had described it.

"What do you think this means?" was all he managed to ask, not letting go of her hand.

"I have no idea, but that is why I thought of these old caves, they too have symbols and I thought maybe they would shed some light on it."

They both looked up at the symbols on the wall again. "They look very similar to the symbols in your bracelet," Josh almost whispered.

Torri nodded. "Yes, you're right. I don't know what this means but I have a strong feeling that Evia may be able to help and that is where I am heading to next."

Joshua asked if he could go with her, it was just he didn't want her to leave him, not just yet. He would have jumped at any excuse to stay in her company. He was fascinated with her story, it was intriguing. It occurred to him that the symbols on her bracelet were not unlike that of Patrick's charm around his neck, which he had always admired. It was all so mysterious, this new commission. He wanted to know more; could it all be connected? She seemed keen on this idea and as she looked up at him they gently kissed. It was spontaneous. She felt drawn to him; it was like magnetism. They couldn't help it; they both felt it and in that kiss they both knew that they had found each other …

Chapter Nineteen

Joshua held Torri's hand as they walked back down the hill towards the coffee booth. No one would have ever guessed that they had only just met, their conversation so easy, like they had known each other always. As they walked, he continued to tell her about his life and passion for old artefacts and their history. She smiled, they had so much in common. He too was passionate and she understood his passion for his work. He noticed that she was smiling and returning the smile, he asked her, "What are you smiling at?"

"You," she replied laughing. "I can't believe that we are here, I am holding your hand and feel like I have known you all my life and yet we have only just met."

He stopped and stepped in front of her smiling. "Me too," he said as he pulled her gently towards him and they kissed again. Like the old cliché, time seemed to stand still; they were lost in each other. No past, present or future existed, just the two of them.

When at last they could pull themselves away from each other, Joshua whispered, "Where have you been all of my life?" and they both laughed, both feeling that they wanted to explode with the love that consumed them. The bracelet on Torri's wrist seemed to be glowing brighter as they continued their journey down the hill, their arms wrapped around each other. Josh smiled to himself. How was he going to explain this one to Patrick …?

The coffee booth was in view and Joshua was hoping that Evia would be on duty, Torri told him not to worry and that she would be there. "It's strange, but she is always there when I need to talk to her, it's as if she knows" They could smell the aroma of the coffee as they approached, "Oh, smells good" Josh uttered, he loved his coffee as did Torri, coffee had lasted through all the changes and had not been lost to the modern world. They both hurried to get inside, the air was turning chilly outside and it had just started to rain again, the weather was very strange at the moment and the atmosphere had a strange odour not unlike sulphur. Their pace quickened as they got near to the door, trying to avoid getting too wet. They almost fell through the door, both laughing as they steadied themselves. Evia greeted them as they entered. "Welcome, Torri and Joshua. I am so pleased that you have met at last." She smiled at them both. They both looked at each other, puzzled, wondering what she meant, she didn't seem at all surprised to see them together; it was as if she was expecting them.

She beckoned them both over to a couple of comfortable seats near the window. "Sit yourselves down there and get warm. I will bring you over a couple of nice coffees with maybe a cookie or two," she said warmly winking at Torri. Josh fleetingly noticed that the coffee booth was empty again but the thought quickly passed, he had other distractions. They sat themselves down, Joshua pulling his chair close to Torri's; he wanted her close to him. Almost immediately Evia came over with two coffees and two extremely large cookies. Joshua's eyes widened; he had never seen cookies like these before, they certainly weren't the standard issue supplied by T.R.I.G.O.M.

"Freshly baked by myself today." Evia smiled. Could she read his thoughts? he wondered. As he took a bite the flavour of chocolate mixed with an almond taste exploded in his mouth stimulating taste buds that he was sure he had never experienced before, particular with the bland food that everyone had gotten used to. He hadn't realised how hungry he had suddenly become as he greedily took another bite wanting more of the flavours and texture of this delicious cookie. Evia smiled at him as she saw the delight on his face. They both sipped the hot coffee, feeling the warmth of the delicious strong liquid as they drank and Joshua wrapped his hands around his cup to warm his hands, which had just started to go blue with the cold. He shivered a little as the warmth started to seep through. They both took a bite of their cookies which induced an "Mmmmm" from both of them at the same time, causing them both to laugh out loud.

"It's nice to see two smiling faces." Evia smiled.

Josh couldn't help but ask about the cookies. "Where did you get the ingredients from for these delicious cookies? They are like nothing I have ever tasted before."

Evia didn't answer his question, instead she just smiled as she sat herself down and looked at them both with such warmth, like a mother would look at her children. "You have found each other," she said very calmly and held both their hands. They both looked at her quizzically but she just smiled. They could both feel the love that she was emanating. They both felt secure and safe in this place talking to this woman who they didn't really know too much about but at the same time it was as if they had known her too all their lives. For some time they all sat there in silence enjoying the ambience, no questions or worries, just absorbing the tranquillity and love that was in the room. It was like a magical spell being woven around them and no one wanted to break it.

Evia eventually broke the silence. "You wanted to talk to me, Torri?"

She nodded but wasn't too sure how to begin. She showed her the bracelet and re-told the events of the strange evening that had brought it to her. After she had finished recalling the events there was a few moments silence before Evia spoke …

Chapter Twenty

Patrick made his way back to the hotel, his mind pondering on all the events of the last few weeks. It seemed that the more he tried to make sense of them, the less he understood and he only ended up with more unanswered questions. He looked around him as he walked and started to reflect. The world was certainly a different place from the decades that his grandparents would have known. Nano technology had played a major part in the technological discoveries that had taken place, particular in cures for serious illness and the structure and control of D.N.A. Perhaps, as some thought, these leaps forward in this field had come too quickly. Human kind struggled to integrate some of the radical change into everyday social and behavioural aspects, creating a detached and superficial culture. Computers and Artificial Intelligence-enhanced beings seemed to take over the most fundamental functions, whilst people became more and more reliant on them, eventually losing any interest or inclination to do things on their own or of a physical nature. However, although artificial intelligence was now self-generating and evolving, the council still consisted of humans whose responsibilities were to monitor and check that protocols were not being broken. This gave confidence to those who had concerns, that the council still had the ultimate control over all the network and intelligence units that existed. Patrick, himself, often wondered how long the council would remain in its current form and although he had been born into this modern world, he liked individuality and the ability to be creative. He believed that this was the essence of mankind and if this were to be lost what would the world become?

His reflections now turned to Egypt as it too had greatly changed in both its climate and culture. The hot deserts no longer existed because it had become colder and much wetter, in contrast to other parts of the world which had become hot and arid, making life difficult for some. T.R.I.G.O.M. had taken over the Egyptian road systems and building structures. Poverty did not exist in the same way of old, as money was not used and housing structures known as cells were provided for everyone, complete with full technical facilities. No one needed their own transport, although designated personal vehicles were still optional, otherwise you just programmed in your requirements and a vehicle would arrive outside your door to transport you to your destination. There was no congestion, people didn't want to travel, there was no need to as everything was at hand in their cells or provided for by T.R.I.G.O.M. Traffic on the road was light and there was no waiting or having to share with strangers, unless you chose to. Human contact had grown less and less. It was unusual for someone to actually have physical contact with another, unless it was absolutely necessary. The art of conversation was certainly not what it used to be, modern language now only consisting of short abbreviated words which had evolved in many areas to what would seem a completely foreign language to those from another time. People were able to look as young as they wished, whilst muscles and strength were frowned upon and not encouraged. Nano technology had been controlled and developed to treat and eradicate cancers, a deadly disease of many decades. Spinal and bone diseases were all rectified by Nano bots, entering the body and targeting specific areas. Yes, advancement was a wonderful thing, Patrick thought. He shivered a little as he considered life in another hundred years!

Chapter Twenty-One

Patrick had chosen to walk back to the hotel in order to try and shake off this dull headache that seemed to have become more persistent. The walk had tired him but there was just one more thing he had to do before going back for a badly needed rest. Patrick was not a person to greatly believe in magic or mystical premonitions, he neither believed nor disbelieved and it was just something he never gave much thought to, only perhaps in the context of its influence on ancient civilisations. As he was walking back, displaying his usual habit of holding his golden charm, he had the strongest feeling to ensure its safety. He decided to detour back to his car and again opened the hidden compartment within it. He took off his chain holding the golden charm and placed it within the metal box that Admar had given him. He was not exactly sure why he had done it but he felt better having done so with a certainty that he had done the right thing. Its absence around his neck made him feel strangely vulnerable and unprotected, he was glad to step inside the hotel lobby as if it was safer to be inside than out. He shivered again as the dark clouds thickened and the cold started to creep into his bones. The hotel's personalised bot greeted him as he entered, ready to cater for any needs that he may have had. He dismissed the bot and made his way to his room. The door opened automatically for him, immediately recognising his D.N.A. Once he got inside, he looked at his computer visual screen which had automatically turned on as he had entered the room. Every person had access to their personal data system, whatever time and where ever they were in the world. He noticed that he had received an auto visual message whilst he had been out. Realising that he had not taken his personal office pad, "POP" out with him, he instructed the computer to play the message. The official opening symbol made him sit up; this symbol only appeared on official messages received from T.R.I.G.O.M. itself. The "Hubot" appeared on the screen. It was T.R.I.G.O.M.'s latest version which had a human-looking face but a metallic body which pulsated as it spoke. The voice was deep and precise. Patrick hated the sound of these "machines". With all the great leaps forward, they still lacked emotion even though their facial structures were flexible and able to imitate expressions. The Hubot spoke.

"We hope you are having a nice stay in Atbara and would request that you visit our base in the city centre. We wish to discuss the nature of your visit here. A vehicle will be sent for you within half an hour of you arriving back at your hotel." The message ended. Patrick realised that the hotel's computer would have sent the necessary message that he had arrived back in his room and sat back for a moment. What was that all about? he wondered, feeling uneasy. Why would T.R.I.G.O.M. want to know about his visit? Was that the real reason or was there an ulterior motive? His mind began to go into overdrive until he took a deep breath and reprimanded himself for his paranoia. He went to touch his charm, feeling a sudden panic when he realised it wasn't around his neck. Why did he take it off? He questioned himself; he wished now for its comfort, something which he had always felt when he touched it. He started to try and rationalise this request and to try and calm himself down. He reminded himself that he was classed as a free person and had the right to travel and work where ever he chose, they probably were just welcoming him or doing random checks, nothing to worry about. There were a few individuals who were not free to do as they wished. This modern world was not completely free of crime or disorder, they were strictly controlled by T.R.I.G.O.M. and should they become too troublesome, they had a habit of just disappearing from society. Sadly no one now questioned these sudden disappearances from general society. On the surface it seemed that no one cared but perhaps more tragically people were too isolated and withdrawn into their own world to notice. Patrick, however, wondered on a darker note that even if people did notice these strange disappearances, would they dare to investigate? Again, it was taken for granted that T.R.I.G.O.M. looked after everything and knew the best course of action for any trouble makers. There were areas, known as the "red zones" scattered around the world and at all Air Disc Stations. These were places that people who were unauthorised to travel or people that had restrictions and had dared to be where they should not be were taken. Patrick had no idea what was in these places or what happened to the people that were taken to them. The few people he had dared speak about it to, also knew nothing. It was a subject people were uncomfortable with, and so he never pursued it to any great depths. The General Information Units around the world provided by T.R.I.G.O.M. were also not forthcoming with information about these areas and any questions asked, would generate a reply as "No information available – T.R.I.G.O.M. classified."

Patrick did not want to antagonise his current situation and knew that it would be pointless to generate an information "request" to find out exactly why he was being summoned, so he decided to sit and wait for the transportation vehicle to arrive and take him to the city. After all, what had he to hide? He was here on a working vacation with his friend, exploring their mutual interests in ancient artefacts and historical sites. He decided against letting Josh know just yet as any messages could be intercepted and he didn't want to bring Josh into their observations until he knew what it was all about.

Chapter Twenty-Two

Evia's first words were, "Josh how is your arm?" Josh looked a little taken aback, he wasn't aware that she knew about his arm and it was not what he was expecting to hear. Torri looked at him, puzzled. He explained briefly about the accident and as he was telling them, he took off his coat and rolled up his sleeve so that they could both see his arm.

"How did you know about my arm?" he asked, looking at Evia. His arm looked sore where the skin was red and swollen. Within the redness, there were small blue lines, just like a tattoo as he had described it to Patrick. As he looked again, the blue lines looked larger, appearing more like symbols.

Torri gasped. "Look, they are like the symbols in the bracelet." Josh looked again at her wrist and indeed the glowing symbols seemed to be very similar to the lines on his arm. As they looked at the bracelet, each symbol appeared, as before, one after the other, each fading away to allow them to see the next one.

"What the hell is happening?" Josh's voice got louder with the sheer panic he was feeling.

Evia turned to them calmly. "Please do not be afraid, all will become clear. In time you will know all that there is to know, but for now it is too dangerous to know everything and so I am here to guide you. You both have an important role to play in the evolution of mankind and there is someone else I would like you to speak with. Your friend Patrick, has already met him," she looked at Josh, "and you have too very briefly, Josh. He is the man that you felt touch your arm at the hospital, his name is Admar."

Josh breathed in heavily and Torri couldn't stop herself from shaking, she wasn't sure if it was the cold or the fear. Josh took her hand and held it tightly in his for reassurance as Evia continued. "A great change is about to happen. The last time such an important change took place, it was recorded by ancient writings, the Bible, the Koran, Holy Scriptures, they each record the same events and that was the purpose of their existence, to record events. It is a time for the planet to change again but our bodies of flesh will not be able to protect our human essence during this change and so they must be protected. It will not be a place that you would recognise as Earth during this transformation. Make no mistake, it is not for Robots to take over," she smiled at this concept, "but our physical form will evolve when everything is ready. The symbols that you have on your arm and in your bracelet contain special codes for DNA modifications but they are also a key to unlock the vessel which will enable you to carry out your destiny." She smiled. "I do not expect you to understand at the moment or know how this will happen but there are more pressing tasks to do first. First you must get to the Great Pyramid and the specific stone as Admar has given instructions to Patrick."

She looked at Josh but before he could utter a word, Torri gasped and almost shouted, "WHAT? I have been given just such an assignment from T.R.I.G.O.M."

Evia looked troubled. "Then we can waste no more time, no time for further explanations as T.R.I.G.O.M. cannot be allowed to interfere with the events that must come to pass. To them it will seem like a threat to their existence even though they do not know how. They know only the way they have chosen and it would seem that they are already aware of more than we had hoped."

Josh was the first to compose himself. "But how are we both important and what about Patrick? We are just everyday people, leading usual lives."

Again Evia smiled. "I think you both know that you are not. You were born for the roles you will undertake, chosen from the time this Earth was formed. You both have always felt different, not accepting this world of inactive people, who are reliant on artificial intelligence and Avatar worlds but you prefer, instead, the outdoors and so appreciating the real essence of this world. Your personalities and preferences have not developed by accident and they are your tools to help you as you head towards your destiny which is a destiny that you both chose a very long time ago."

She then looked at Torri. "You have always known that you are different, with the special gifts you possess, although perhaps not fully understanding why you have them."

Torri nodded. Just then Admar came into the coffee booth, his face white and troubled.

Chapter Twenty-Three

As predicted, the official vehicle from T.R.I.G.O.M. arrived at the hotel to collect Patrick. He was ready and waiting. He had been pacing the floor in his room, his nerves starting to get the better of him, agitated further by the absence of his lucky charm. Keep calm, keep calm, he told himself over and over again. It was crucial in order to get through this; he knew he would be monitored. He still wasn't quite sure why he had been summoned and could only connect it to the strange events of recent weeks. The holographic hotel facilitator appeared in his room to inform him that he was required in the lobby. His door opened and the red moving strip was ready and waiting for him. He smiled to himself, yes he really was being summoned and he certainly would be foolish to put up any resistance although he had a very strong urge to just take to his heels and run until he could run no more. Controlling this urge, he stepped on to the base of the strip as calmly as he could, which immediately activated and transported him to the waiting vehicle. It was a very spacious and comfortable vehicle and as he sat down in it, the seat moulded perfectly to his body for his safety. He felt uncomfortable and confined with a nagging thought at the back of his mind that it was more of a restraint than required for any safety purposes. The vehicle's scanning device activated, he knew he was being checked over by the computer, the chip in his arm providing information as it was being scanned. He decided he would carry on as normally as possible and asked the purpose of this visit, directing the question to the on-board computer. The synthetic voice response from the vehicle was as he had expected. "This information is T.R.I.G.O.M. classified." Realising he was going to get no more answers, he decided to remain quiet for the rest of the journey. Still frantically trying to keep his stress levels down he made himself take deep long breaths and it was only the low humming of the vehicle which invaded the silence of the journey. His thoughts began to wander to the task that he and Josh had been given. The Great Pyramid and that certain stone seemed to be very important. He had hidden away the container and instructions that Admar had given him, he had felt it prudent to do so and although rooms at the hotel were supposed to be private and secure, he did not completely feel at ease with this and even as a small boy, he had not trusted artificial intelligence and the motivations behind some of the technologies that had evolved. Now that he had been summoned by T.R.I.G.O.M., he was glad of his actions but why did he have this feeling of uneasiness which seemed to be getting stronger? The journey to the Atbara headquarters only took ten minutes even though it was some way from the hotel. The speed allotted to his vehicle was greater than the speed allotment for many of the day to day journey requirements and so he did not have long to reflect upon events and the purpose of this visit. The vehicle arrived at the main office gates, which opened upon their approach. They proceeded slowly. Patrick looked to his left and saw the ominous Red Zone, they seemed to have them at all the T.R.I.G.O.M. headquarters and disc stations. The vehicle started to slow as it passed this zone making Patrick's heart start to quicken but the vehicle carried on. It stopped when it reached a large door, the visitor section. Patrick breathed a sigh of relief. The door of the vehicle opened and Patrick was greeted by the section's IBOT. Patrick was seated on a transportation chair which started to move down a long but well lit corridor. It seemed to Patrick that he was heading downwards, all natural light seemed to cease and only the artificial light remained. The chair was designed to carry its occupant in comfort to the required destination without any physical exertion. It was comfortable and moulded to his body just like the seat had done so in the car, ensuring he was secure. It gave him the same feeling as before that he would not be able to get out of it should he want to. The chair headed towards a set of large metal looking doors and as he approached he thought he was going to smash straight into them.

The chair didn't stop, instead they just dissolved in front of him. His heart was pounding. He now found himself in a very large room, full of large visual screens and the far wall was lined with stationary Hubots, the latest robotic creation. The chair relaxed its grip and Patrick was able to shift position. His body had been tense creating a cramp in his leg. He moved his hand to rub the sore area, easing the cramp as his body became more relaxed. A couple of minutes elapsed and then he heard someone enter the room. He was greeted by a tall man, dressed in the customary blue T.R.I.G.O.M. uniform. Patrick recognised the senior ranking holographic strip on his arm as that from the main security sector. Patrick looked up at him, he felt slightly relieved, at least he looked human and he would not have to deal with a robot of any sorts. He smiled and told Patrick, rather firmly, to remain seated but offered him his hand and introduced himself as Braedan, a class one ranking T.R.I.G.O.M. council member. He asked Patrick if he would like a beverage, which he politely declined. He was far too nervous, he had begun to feel a little sick and his head had started to throb.

Chapter Twenty-Four

Braedan was a tall man and as age was a hard thing to determine these days, with gene technology able to prolong the ageing process and other cosmetic advancements, Patrick could only guess that he was older than he looked. The only thing that stood out was his eyes, a bright piercing blue that seemed to look right through you. Patrick thought he looked vaguely familiar and he displayed quite a pleasant manner which helped ease Patrick's growing nerves. "I trust your journey was comfortable?" Braedan asked, smiling. Patrick felt those piercing blue eyes staring at him and although his face smiled, his eyes remained cold and expressionless. He still had that unnerving feeling that he had met him somewhere before. Patrick composed himself, he must act as if nothing was wrong and tried to imagine how he would have felt had the other strange events of the past weeks had not taken place. He concluded that he would be quite annoyed and extremely put out at this inconvenience and intrusion on his precious time and so he answered with the most confident tone to his voice he could muster.

"The journey was fine thank you, as would be expected by T.R.I.G.O.M.," he replied, adding a slightly annoyed edge to his voice. "However, I do not understand the purpose of this visit which has interrupted my leisure time."

Braedan, again displayed that emotionless smile. "I am sorry that this may seem like an inconvenience, however it was necessary so that we can update our data and clarify some concerns which have come to our attention."

Patrick frowned. "Perhaps you would like to enlighten me so that we can proceed and we can both get back to our own business."

"Ah, business." Braedan latched on to his last word as if it was an offence. "You seem in a hurry to get back, is there a problem?"

"Nnno," Patrick stuttered a little with his reply, "but I am on leisure time and I want to make the most of it."

"Or perhaps your friend Joshua will wonder where you are?" This time Braedan did not try to smile and Patrick stiffened at this remark.

"Yes I am here with my friend who you seem to know about, is there a problem?" He returned the question to Braedan but taking out the harshness in his voice and adding a softer tone. He was beginning to realise that he could be in serious danger here and was trying not to antagonise this man who gave him the feeling he was more than he first appeared to be.

Braedan responded. "Maybe not, however, we must enquire as to the nature of your visit here to Atbara. We check all visitors as you know and do random background checks as desired. We found that your personal chip seems to have lost some data going back a couple of weeks. Because of this I was curious and decided to check your whereabouts up to the point the data was lost. We discovered that you were in the village of Doolin and although it was only a few hours lost we found it odd and so I would request that you shed some light on this matter."

Patrick had noticed Braedan's change of tense. It was usually plural when talking for the council but he had clearly used I as if it was him personally who wanted to know. Braedan continued. "These chips are designed to withstand a nuclear explosion and yet its signal was blocked and we have no data."

Patrick's mind raced. Yes big brother is certainly watching and he knew exactly when it must have been; his visit to the old cliffs of Moher, his secret meeting with Admar and Evia inside the Doolin Caves where he seemed to have been taken to another place. Patrick composed himself and answered as calmly as possible. He tried to appear puzzled and answered, "How odd. I am sure that I do not have a clue, I am not technically minded, as I am sure you are aware, my field of expertise is in old relics not modern ones," he joked, making a light comment and hoping it would ease the tension that seemed to have developed in the room.

Sadly his attempt at humour was lost on Braedan. "Ah yes, you and your friend are well known within that field. So what interests you in Atbara?"

Patrick was now feeling a little more confident and so went on to explain that he and Josh were just here to relax, more so for Josh who was recovering from a road accident and that they both felt they could have a leisurely look at the old buildings and maybe visit Egypt, the place of the old pyramids, structures which they had both always been interested in. To them this was relaxing as they enjoyed visiting the old structures and liked to speculate on their history. Braedan showed no emotion, although Patrick could have sworn that his eyes flickered slightly when he mentioned the old pyramids and Josh's accident but he seemed to listen intently as Patrick continued. "We don't intend to stay too long just enough to recharge the old batteries so to speak."

"You are both unusual in the fact that you like the outdoors and physical activities," Braedan said.

"That is not a crime as yet, as far as I am aware," Patrick stated.

"Not as yet," he seemed to linger on those words, "but we still have not established why your chip has malfunctioned and you do not seem to have given me a satisfactory explanation."

"That is because I do not know the answer, but if I did I would obviously tell you. I think I would like to go now." Patrick was beginning to get angry. A feeling that was tinged with a cold foreboding feeling.

"For the time being that will not be possible. We will have to check your chip and investigate this matter further. There is also the question of an old charm that was detected around your neck on your arrival to Egypt, which is of interest to us but I see you are no longer wearing it. Could you tell me where that is right now?"

Patrick's heart began to pound in his chest to the point he thought it was going to explode. His charm, why would anyone be interested in it? He suddenly knew beyond doubt he had done the right thing but how was he going to explain its absence ...? He knew he had to lie and risk being detected. "I have misplaced it but I am sure it is somewhere in my hotel room, but why would you be interested in my old charm which I have had since boyhood?"

Braedan just looked at him, devoid of any emotion, his piercing blue eyes looking right through him sending a chill down his spine. The chair he had been sitting in gripped him tightly and one of the Hubots from the far wall suddenly activated, its blue light glowing through its body. Braedan turned to it. "Escort our guest to the Red zone ..."

Chapter Twenty-Five

Admar came rushing over to them. "We have a problem."

Evia looked at him with concern. "What has happened?" she asked.

"Patrick has been taken by T.R.I.G.O.M. for questioning, they have taken him to the Red Zone, and so we must act quickly."

"The charm," Evia whispered as she put her hands to her forehead and for the first time, Josh noticed that she didn't look so calm.

Josh got up quickly, nearly knocking Torri over in his haste but Admar put his hands on his shoulder. "We must act quickly but we cannot attract any attention, Patrick will be safe for the time being. There has to be a slight change of plan, you and Torri must go to the stone, then we can deal with the other situation."

Evia smiled at them now. "You two were meant to go there together and Patrick has another role to play."

"I do not have the container or instructions, Patrick had those." Josh looked at them both in panic.

"We have no time to get another container, do you think that he would have them with him?" Admar asked him.

Josh tried to think, he knew his old friend very well, enough to know that he would have most likely put them safe. He had no trust in T.R.I.G.O.M. and he would have thought this a big adventure, just like the books he often spoke of. He shook his head. "No he would have put them safe."

"Think, Joshua, where would he have put them?"

His mind was so full he just could not think. Admar looked at Torri, she put her hands to his forehead and he felt a wave of calmness almost immediately. She closed her eyes and told him to concentrate. Suddenly he could see Patrick very clearly, he could hear Torri's voice, gently soothing him in the background and then in a flash he opened his eyes. "I know where they are."

Her job done, Torri stepped back and took her hands from his forehead. He grabbed them back and kissed each hand tenderly.

He had remembered their journey to Atbara and that they had travelled in Patrick's own vehicle. Although only a few people had self-allotted vehicles, choosing to use them only when they were required, Patrick was one of the few. It had made Josh laugh on many occasions, knowing all vehicles were self-cleaning and maintenance free but Patrick would still insist on spending hours tinkering and wiping it over, just like they used to do with the old cars of the past. "It's in the car," he whispered to Admar.

He nodded and said, "Come we must go, it is starting to get dark and no doubt the streets will be full of surveillance drones and maybe more than we would like to see near the hotel. They will have scanned his room and all his belongings, although I do not think that they know what they are looking for."

"Well, why is the stone so important?" Torri asked.

"We will talk later as we have not got much time and you must hurry."

"Are you not coming with us?" Josh looked at both Evia and Admar quizzically.

"It is for you and Torri to go alone. Once you are there we will find you. We cannot stay in the outside world for too long." Evia spoke softly but firmly.

With no other explanation forthcoming, Josh and Torri recognised the urgency in her voice and hurriedly they both pulled on their coats and headed for the door.

"Remember, you have done nothing wrong. Torri you are about your usual business and Joshua you are a visitor. You are friends, there is nothing wrong with that so please try to look more relaxed in case you draw attention to yourselves. We don't know how much they know." Admar spoke softly just before they went through the door. They looked back at him and tried to smile as they acknowledged his words.

Josh took Torri's hand as they stepped into the cool air. It had begun to get dark just as Admar had said, but the rain had stopped and a cool breeze had picked up. They walked in the direction of the hotel trying to act as normal as possible. They could see the surveillance drones patrolling overhead, ready to report any unusual activity and making sure all was quiet. They both began to feel like they were being watched, perhaps just imagination with their own thoughts triggering a degree of paranoia, however both of them felt these feelings more intensely as they approached the hotel. Josh noticed a drone starting to turn their way and instinctively grabbed Torri pushing her behind one of the large trees leading up the drive of the hotel. They were lucky that this was one of the remaining areas where trees were left to grow in peace. Thankfully it protected them and provided an adequate hiding place to avoid being detected. The drone had not noticed them and continued on its usual path. They both let out a sigh of relief, Josh looked at Torri, the moonlight shining on her face and he thought how beautiful she was. He wanted to hold her so badly. They hadn't had a chance to be together alone and he didn't know now whether that chance would ever come. She looked back at him and smiled but noticed the sadness in his eyes. She felt it too but they had no time to dwell on it. "Come on," he whispered as he composed himself. "The vehicle stacking tube is around the back, we should keep under the cover of the trees but if we are stopped we are just on the way back to my accommodation room and you are my guest."

"Why thank you, I would love to be your guest." Torri looked at him with a mischievous glint in her eyes. They both laughed which helped to relieve some of their tension. They took in deep breaths and continued on quickly towards the metal disc showing the location of the vehicle tube.

Chapter Twenty-Six

Vehicles were placed in an automated stacking tube which then descended far below ground level, the position marked with a transparent plate above ground. When a vehicle was required, the relevant vehicle would be retrieved and delivered back up by the robotic system, up through the transparent plate, checked and ready to go. Vehicles that were for "sole use," such as Patrick's, were retrieved by DNA recognition by the sole user. Another person could request the vehicle if prior authorisation had been given. Patrick had told Josh on their journey to Atbara, that the vehicle had scanned his DNA so that he would be able to use the vehicle if he wished. Although at the time, Josh had thought it very unlikely as he had only planned on travelling with Patrick or walking to the required sites of interest as needed, he was glad now of this forethought by Patrick.

As they approached the stacking tube, they stopped just at the edge where, through the transparent plate they could see the vehicles below. The plate was slightly larger than the length of a vehicle and all the vehicles were stacked in the circular tube, so many on one level working down the tube. This greatly reduced the space required for dormant vehicles, they could hold so many. As this was a relatively small hotel and surrounding area, the stacking tube was not one of the largest, most of the spaces were empty. People certainly didn't travel like they used to, partly due to adverse climate changes and preferring instead to stay at home, where any business could be conducted. The Avatar community was ever expanding, where many chose to escape and lead their lives within safe and controlled parameters.

The retrieval panel for the stacking tube rose up on their approach, detecting their arrival with efficiency. It had a circular visual unit, surrounded by luminous colour controls. The visual unit glowed and the virtual keeper appeared on the screen and proceeded to go through its pre-set programme. "If you wish to place a vehicle please look at the red dial. If you wish to retrieve a vehicle please look at the green dial. Any other requirements please speak now." Josh and Torri looked at each other, hoping that no new security protocols had been initiated. Well here goes, Josh thought and looked at the green dial. As he looked at the dial it began to glow, scanning his DNA for recognition. There was a slight pause and they both held their breath. The virtual keeper appeared again. "Your vehicle is ready for you please stand in the designated area to ensure your safety." Greatly relieved that there didn't seem to be a problem, they stepped on to the sensor plate ready to receive the vehicle. As soon as the sensor plates were activated, the transparent plate covering the stacking tube disappeared and within minutes Patrick's vehicle moved upwards, secure on a metallic holding disc. As soon as it was level on the ground its doors opened for boarding. Josh and Torri got quickly into the vehicle, conscious that its movements could be detected and controlled by T.R.I.G.O.M. should anything suspicious be detected. The on board computer requested instructions for movement and clearance control. Josh requested the car to move to the side of the accommodation and initiate shut down mode until further instructions. The vehicle moved as requested and the transparent plate once again covered the stacking tube. As soon as the vehicle had stopped and shut down mode had been initiated, Josh looked down towards the dash of the vehicle. He put his hand on the metal dash putting pressure on the metal as he moved it along, trying to find the trigger point of the compartment that he had seen Patrick use. After a few seconds which seemed like an eternity, the compartment opened. Quickly Josh put his hand inside searching for the metal case that he had seen Patrick put there. His hand hit something hard, he grabbed it and pulled it out. It was indeed the black case for which they were looking for, he didn't try to open it, he knew that they had no time to waste. He turned to Torri. "We must try and get to the pyramid before they have

88

cause to think that anything is wrong, but I don't suggest that we use the car. Is it far from here?"

"It is quite a way. We could go via the Nile up past the Nasser Lake. I know it well. Many years ago it would have taken at least a day to reach Giza but there are 'shoot tube' routes which have not been used over the last few decades. I have an old subboat, the first of its kind all those years ago, which belonged to my great grandfather. It is hidden away as all the old form of travel should have been scrapped many years ago. I just could not get rid of it, my grandfather loved this boat, which his father had given him, he told me to keep it safe."

She caught her breath for a moment as the tears welled up in her eyes, wondering if he knew that she would need it so urgently one day. Josh held her close understanding her grief. They clung together for a few precious moments but their mission was becoming urgent. They looked up at the dark skies as they heard a low rumbling sound in the distance. A storm was setting in and the darkness of the night was devouring what was left of the day, they needed to move. Torri explained that not many drones patrolled the rivers and as these boats were no longer used it would be unlikely that they would be looking for anything like it, they would be well hidden under the water.

"Come on then, quickly, let's get going," Josh said urgently. He held the case tightly and grabbed her hand. "We will look at the instructions on the way but we should leave here quickly, the weather looks like it's about to change too."

A large flash of lightning lit the skies and that smell of sulphur was getting more pungent. Josh turned to go but Torri stopped him. "Wait," she turned to look at Josh, "we must put the vehicle back into its parking slot. We don't want to draw attention to Patrick's vehicle, which would happen if we leave it here."

Josh nodded, knowing that she was right. They couldn't just abandon it here, it would be detected very quickly and would send out alarm signals, if it hadn't already. They both jumped into the vehicle and instructed it back to the stacking tube. The panel rose up again ready for the parking procedure as they approached. The vehicle went efficiently on to the awaiting platform, allowing Josh and Torri to get out safely and initiate the parking procedure. They had decided to ensure that the parking process was completed successfully but Torri had insisted that they take cover behind the accommodation boundary wall out of sight. She explained that it was one of her feelings which she had learned not to ignore but assured Josh that it was just a precaution. However, it was not long after they had taken cover that Torri nudged Josh and pointed over to the far left. One of the T.R.I.G.O.M. overhead probes had appeared suddenly accompanied by six Hubots, who were approaching the stacking tube alarmingly fast, with their red lights flashing angrily. Torri took Josh's hand and whispered, "Quickly we must get to the boat."

Chapter Twenty-Seven

Braedan had accompanied Patrick on his journey to the Red Zone. Patrick felt himself shaking as Braedan turned back round to face him, the Hubot's red light glowing behind him. Patrick knew that they would have been monitoring his vital signs, indicating his stress levels, which he was convinced would have hit extreme levels at this point. "I do not think you have any cause to take this action, I have told you everything that I can. I am not responsible for this chip if it's not working." Patrick almost shouted his protest at Braedan.

"Do you know anyone by the name of Admar by any chance?" He looked coldly into Patrick's eyes and even though he was completely thrown by his knowledge of Admar he replied as coldly as he could.

"Who I know or do not know is my business and I cannot even comprehend as to why who I know should concern you or why you think it to be any of your business." Patrick seemed to have mustered up his courage, fear seeming to subside and real anger surfacing to take its place.

"You forget, that everything is our business if we feel that anyone or anything could jeopardise any fundamental operation or threaten the integrity of the security of T.R.I.G.O.M. and its council. It becomes my business, under the heading of S.E.C.U.R.I.T.Y." He spoke the last words harshly and precisely, pronouncing each letter as he came right up to Patrick's face. The Hubot which was standing directly behind him also moved closer. Patrick's hand went automatically to his neck for the comfort of his faithful old charm. It wasn't there and Braedan smiled. Suddenly the chair began to vibrate and the floor just dissolved beneath him. He felt the chair start to descend quickly downwards through it, entering a dark tunnel. Patrick could only see the glow from the Hubot which was accompanying him on his journey. He felt numb with fear as the chair moved faster and faster downwards. He started to feel nauseous with the speed he was travelling at; feeling that at any moment he would be sick. Just as he was about to lose his battle with his sickness it stopped suddenly as it reached its destination: the Red Zone!

The chair released him and by instinct he shot up but the Hubot was right in front of him, its blue light radiating as it changed to a deep red glow. Did he imagine it or did it appear even more menacing as it instructed him to take a couple of steps forward on to a moving floor? The floor proceeded forward but it still felt like he was heading downwards. He was disorientated and so could not be sure. He hardly dared look around him but as he looked to his left, he saw what looked like large cylindrical shapes, not unlike large test tubes, but they must have been at least ten feet in height and filled with a yellowy looking substance. He wanted to look closer but the Hubot put its cold metallic hand on his back, telling him to look forward in its emotionless voice. They were travelling faster now and Patrick found it hard to focus on anything. He was starting to feel nauseous again as he descended lower into the dark. After what seemed like an eternity he could feel himself slowing down and then he felt something warm and soft touching his feet. It was working its way up his body; it covered his legs, he couldn't move. He tried to look down but found that he couldn't; only through the corner of his eye could he make out something silvery covering his arm and working up towards his face. It felt like soft but icily cold fingers caressing his skin. His heart was pounding and he was struggling for breath. He felt his body move and he seemed to be hanging, suspended in mid-air. He couldn't move any of his muscles, he could only control the movement of his eyes which widened in terror as he saw what looked like silvery spindly cords coming towards him completely engulfing his body. He felt searing pain like he had never felt before as the cord penetrated his skull, his head becoming numb and heavy. He thought he was going to pass out with the pain and the intensity of discomfort which was increasing rapidly. He was hanging upright and felt himself being lowered down slightly until Braedan was directly in front of him looking straight into his eyes. "We will soon know all there is to know about your lost time. You're connected to T.R.I.G.O.M., your brain fully connected now so that we will be able to extract the information that we need," Braedan said with a false smile that made Patrick shiver. "We already know where you have put your charm and I have sent my Hubots out to retrieve it. That was clever as we never considered your vehicle, our mistake."

How did he know about his lucky charm? The thought was fleeting, he was feeling too sick to concentrate on anything. The cords around his body were not covering his mouth so he tried to speak, but the words did not come out of his mouth, instead his words echoed back at him from across this cell-like room, sounding metallic in tone, nothing like Patrick's own voice. "What is happening to me?" came back the computerised version of his question. No feeling in it, just automated in its structure.

Braedan smiled again. "As I told you, Patrick, you are attached to T.R.I.G.O.M. and all your functions are now under its control. Your brain activity is being downloaded for analysis."

Patrick could sense Braedan's satisfaction. "How can you do this? I have not done anything, you have no right."

Braedan spoke to T.R.I.G.O.M. in a language that Patrick had never heard before. Patrick tried to cry out but found he could speak no more and then there was silence. Patrick could sense Braedan's frustration as he watched his face cloud over with a heavy frown as he looked at Patrick. "It appears that we are having difficulties extracting certain information. How can that be?" he said, in no more than a whisper.

He spoke again to T.R.I.G.O.M., this time his voice tinged with anger and the computer spoke back in the same strange language. Patrick wanted to scream with the pain in his head but nothing would come out of his mouth. Braedan spoke to him. "We are aware of an ancient prophesy that does not include T.R.I.G.O.M. in the future and I think that you know more about this than you are telling me but how anything could interfere with your brain patterns making it difficult to fully control your brain, I cannot comprehend. But at the same time it is intriguing. Perhaps we need to consider if there is something out there that has technology far more advanced? Perhaps we will need to resort to some more primitive form of extraction, but for now you will remain in suspension until we retrieve this charm to see what properties it has."

Patrick did not have a clue what he was talking about but for a vague memory of his time with Admar and Evia at the cave when he remembered they had touched his head. When he had looked puzzled they told him it was for protection. He had no time to think; darkness overcame him and he was unconscious.

Chapter Twenty-Eight

Josh and Torri quickened their pace as another flash of lightning lit up the sky. "We are nearly there," Torri shouted to Josh as the rumble of thunder grew increasingly louder. They were both growing tired, they had not stopped and now found themselves battling a strong gale force wind which was getting more forceful by the second. Josh was worried about Patrick. Why had he been taken but more importantly what was happening to him? He had made up his mind that he was going to find out whatever it took. They would look at this precious stone but as soon as they had done what they had been asked they would waste no time in heading off to find Patrick. He had a very strong feeling that getting to the pyramids was the utmost priority. He was growing weary of all this mystery and wanted to know exactly what this was all about with the hope that it might end and things would once again be normal, if that could ever be possible now. He could actually feel the fear growing stronger and stronger as they drew nearer to their destination. They were heading towards the banks of the Nile, no longer the river recorded in ancient writings, now the size of a small ocean. In front of them was a large tree. It looked old and withered but covered a wide area with its expanse of aging foliage. Torri didn't stop but disappeared amongst the leaves. He panicked momentarily but then her hand shot out from nowhere and grabbed his, pulling him down through the leaves. Far from falling flat on his face as he was expecting to, he discovered it was the opening to one of the old sub-boat tunnels. He looked to the right and there it was, probably the only one left of its kind. He had never seen anything like it before or even realised that sub-boats had existed, other than in story tablets, provided for fantasy. Torri looked at it with pride. "This was Grandfather's beloved boat." She smiled and touched it lovingly. It was made of a special alloy that did not rust and it gleamed, looking as new as the day it was built.

"Will it still work?" He turned to Torri.

"Yes of course, it does not rely on any source of energy from T.R.I.G.O.M. It is completely independent with its vacuum propelled system, probably one of the many reasons they were abolished," she said with distaste. Her grandfather had been furious and had refused to get rid of it, successfully hiding it away in the one shoot tube which had never been discovered by T.R.I.G.O.M. Special security patrols had been commissioned to destroy all the tubes and boats in existence. It had been unclear at the time why they had been destroyed, but as usual, nobody questioned the authority of T.R.I.G.O.M., it was just accepted. Some of the older generation, however, believed it was because they could not be easily controlled and so posed a security threat to T.R.I.G.O.M. Those of this thinking never openly voiced their opinions for fear of repercussions or being taken to the dreaded Red Zone from which no one ever returned.

It was a bright red and silver colour, looking more like a bullet than the boats he could remember seeing through his story tablet when he had been engrossed in some fantasy or other. She pressed a panel on the side and the top slid back, revealing a leather interior and two large comfortable looking seats. In fact he couldn't believe how big it looked inside compared to having a seemingly small exterior. She laughed at his puzzled expression. "I don't suppose you have ever heard of the Tardis?" He looked at her again puzzled. "Just some old stories passed down through generations of our family, of an old television programme about a time traveller who had a travelling machine called the Tardis. It looked small from the outside but was enormous inside, something to do with quantum physics." She smiled as she stepped in, he quickly followed. The seats were so comfortable but totally unlike the usual seats which moulded to your body. He felt free and totally relaxed, not feeling controlled or monitored by a computer; it was a new experience. Once they were both seated, the top slid back into place, making a hissing noise as it sealed tightly shut. She pressed another button on the small control panel in front of her, a soft green light shone around them, just enough to see clearly in the darkness of the tunnel. The control panel seemed to come to life and the boat made a low vibrating noise. It was obvious she was familiar with all the controls and he looked at her with such pride, leaning over to gently kiss her cheek. She turned to look at him but before she asked he whispered, "Just because." He didn't need to say any more, it was at that moment that she knew he loved her and she loved him and even though they had no time to embrace their love, she felt the power of it giving her strength. They had to act quickly.

The boat was positioned directly over the start pad facing the long dark shoot tube. Torri explained that this sub-boat created a vacuum and that they would literally shoot through the tunnel. The technology was a remarkable feat of self-propulsion which had been invented around the time of 2020 when many had speculated that Alien technology had been involved. It was also a time where people were not kept informed of important issues; everything was kept secret or false information issued. When T.R.I.G.O.M. had become more prominent in 2038, the true origins of this technology had never been divulged, along with the disappearance of a lot of skills and knowledge in the old ways. The tunnel itself had various tubes leading from it but the main one led straight to the Giza Pyramid. This had been a favourite route of her grandfather. She now wondered if he too had visions, it seemed like he had known of these events and prepared well for them. Perhaps this explained why he understood her so well, but he had never shared or confided anything like this to her. It could just be pure coincidence but she believed not, knowing that he would have had his reasons not to confide in her. She touched another dial, and seat bars came down, securing them both in their seats. This took Josh by surprise and he started in panic. She told him not to worry, they would need to be secure as the boat travelled at a high velocity. He relaxed a little. He could now feel the whole vessel vibrating and then suddenly they shot forward, the force throwing his head back into the soft head rest in the back of the chair. All he could see was a blur of lights which aligned the tunnel, the vessel itself triggering them as it approached. He tried to turn his head to look at Torri but his head was rigid against the chair, she squeezed his hand to reassure him that all was well. She had experienced this before but knew that it was frightening to someone who had not. He closed his eyes, willing the boat to get to its destination, so that he could get out. As quickly as it had started they came to a stop and the bar that was holding him firmly, released and raised back up and away into an overhead panel. He let out a long slow breath; he wasn't too sure what to make of this experience, he was just glad that it was over. The top of the vessel let out a hissing noise as it opened, exposing them to the outside air, still under cover with an entrance further up guarded by a large tree, just like the one at the start of their journey. Torri got out of her seat and climbed out, she held out her hand to help him get up.

"You have obviously done this before." He smiled at her. She looked at him and wanted to laugh. He looked a slight shade of green with his hair all over the place.

"It's something you have to get used to, although I have not tried it too often in fear of detection." She couldn't help but smile as she looked at Josh's white face. She had realised it must have been frightening for someone who had never travelled that way before but she had always found it exhilarating. A passion she had shared with her grandfather and something that T.R.I.G.O.M. had not taken away. Perhaps its secrecy added to the delight she always felt on the rare occasions that she dared to use it. It was often after she thought that some injustice had been done that she used the boat; it was her own secret rebellion and always helped with her frustrations.

Josh was feeling a little light on his feet but after taking a few deep breaths he regained his composure. "Where are we?" He looked at Torri. She told him that they were at the exit tunnel, just opposite the Great Pyramid.

Chapter Twenty-Nine

Torri turned to walk away, but Josh impulsively grabbed her hand and pulled her to him and said softly, "Look, it's still dark and we have only a little time to go before it gets light. We need a few moments to rest, we haven't stopped and we will not be able to do whatever it is we have to do without taking a break." He said this with a hint of frustration and Torri looked at him. He looked tired and was still shaken from the boat journey. They were warm and protected from the outside world and he wanted to capture this moment. Who knew from here what was going to happen to them? Unsure if they would ever have the chance to be together, completely alone again he just wanted it to last as long as possible. He didn't have to explain anything, she intuitively knew his thoughts, both sharing the urgency and desire to be together. She looked up at him, those dark brown eyes seemed to look into her soul and melt her heart, every part of her aching for his touch as she gently stroked his cheek, tenderly kissing each eye, then his nose before reaching for his lips. Their lips met in a slow tender kiss as he stroked her hair, pushing it gently from her face as he pulled his lips away briefly to look at her beautiful face. He wanted to savour the moment hoping that time would stand still. His lips met hers again, this time more passionately as the urgency for each other consumed them. Her head moving back as he kissed her neck, her skin so soft to the touch. Looking at her so close to him.

"You are beautiful," he whispered as she moved her fingers up and down his strong arms before he gently gathered her up in his arms, kissing her as he laid her down on the floor which was cushioned by the fallen leaves of the old tree. It was some time later that they both opened their eyes; they had fallen to sleep wrapped in each other's arms. He looked down at her smiling. They had made love like he had never experienced before confirming their deep love for each other knowing that within each other lay their destiny. He began stroking her face which made her smile, delighting in his touch and the intimacy of the moment. Then her smile faded as she turned to him. "We have no more time and we must go but ..." she kissed him again "... whatever happens we will not forget this time, this place. I so love you." Her eyes began to fill with tears; she was suddenly overwhelmed with the emotion of it all, her feeling of love mixed with the fear of losing him to their fate.

He wiped away her tears, understanding and held her face towards him. "I love you too and I know that we will be OK. I am not going to lose you now that I have found you, we will be together always." He kissed her gently. They both knew that they must get dressed and carry on with their task yet all they wanted to do was stay safe in each other's arms, shutting out the events around them. As they dressed Josh turned to her, realising he was hungry. "We could do with something to eat and drink. It's been a long time since we last ate and we certainly need some energy now," he added cheekily.

She smiled and reached for her coat. It had specially designed pockets which she found quite useful for her work. When she needed extra carrying space for her samples, they were deceptively deep and it was surprising how much she could fit into them. She reached in and pulled out two very large cookies and a flat flask with two cups attached, explaining that Evia had given them to her before they left. The flask kept the coffee hot and the cookies were specially made with nourishment to help them sustain their energy.

"Wow, she thinks about everything." Josh smiled. He was amazed that Torri had been able to fit them all in her pocket. He started to tease her trying to put his hands in her pocket to see what else she had got there. She was laughing as she told him to keep his hands to himself. They laughed together, enjoying a brief moment of fun without pressure or worry. They were both very hungry and in need of that hot coffee which they drank thankfully in between eating their special cookies. The cookies and the coffee did their job and they both felt revived but they were so in love, not even the uncertainty of the task before them could spoil their mood. After the cookies had gone and every drop of coffee consumed they sat back replete, gathering their strength to carry on this journey. After scrambling out of the sub-boat entrance and just past the large tree, they had now arrived close to the pyramid. They both agreed that it was about time to actually read the instructions and take a look into the black case.

Chapter Thirty

They found a clear spot beside the boat which they thought a suitable place to open up the case. Just then a hoot of an owl filled the air, sounding so loud in the quietness of early morning that they both jumped. Torri looked around. "That sounds like Ollie," she whispered with surprise.

"Ollie?" Josh looked at her puzzled.

She just smiled. "I'll explain another time." With that she pointed at the case and Josh had no more time to wonder as he opened up the black case holding the container and the instructions. On top of the instructions, Patrick had placed his chain with his "lucky" charm.

"Look at this," Josh shouted. He couldn't believe it as he knew that Patrick would never take off his charm. He had always worn it for as long as Josh had known him. He felt panic and a sudden fear for his friend but knew he had to pull himself together and carry on. Impulsively he quickly slipped the chain over his head. He thought it the safest place for it until he could return it to Patrick but he it made him feel better somehow. Torri also looked concerned and squeezed his hand tenderly, knowing that he was worried about his friend. Time was of the essence; they needed to look at the instructions. There was a diagram of the Great Pyramid with a picture at the top that they both recognised, although with some quite significant differences. The pyramid didn't appear to be made of the decaying stone of today, but it shone like it was made of a very shiny metal. It was placed in unfamiliar surroundings to that of today. Was this from the past, a projection of the future or even a different place all together? Josh wondered.

"Look. That is where the water level is now," Josh said pointing to the diagram. The stone they required was just below the surface, marked in a different colour. Torri got up quickly and went back over to the boat and after a few minutes returned carrying a small metal case. She put it on to the floor and pulled out a couple of underwater belts, the latest in their day back in 2030. Heavy tanks and masks were hardly remembered now, just relics of the past. The belts were light and when activated, created a force field, protecting its wearer and providing enough air to last over six hours before it needed to be replenished.

"Wow," Josh uttered. "You have everything in there. Do you know how to use them?" He knew it was a silly question but it just came out.

"Of course, my grandfather taught me well and I will show you." She looked at him smiling with pride but with a touch of amusement at the astonishment on Josh's face. She checked the air level on the belts, shown in a small cell-like battery attached to each belt. Luckily they were both full.

There was also a small black pouch in the case which held some old tools. They looked ideal for collecting samples of rock. They were very old but in surprisingly good condition, made of a metal that Josh didn't recognise even though he had come across many antique tools in his field of old relics and historical artefacts. He had no time to ponder as Torri was already putting on the belt and preparing herself for the task in hand. She handed the other belt to Josh. As he took the belt he grabbed her, holding her close which took her completely by surprise. He just wanted to hold her close for a few minutes, to keep her safe and away from harm. Events seemed to have completely taken over. He was worried about Patrick. He had found Torri and didn't want to lose her. It was a moment of panic and love combined together, wanting time to stop time just for a few seconds. She too felt this and melted into his arms returning his embrace and holding on to him tightly. They didn't need to say anything and she responded to his gentle kiss.

They both put on their belts as they walked back to the water's edge. They looked over at the pyramid in the distance, not too far away, surrounded by the dark waters of the Nile. The dark of the night was now giving way to the daylight, but the dark clouds gathering overhead kept the light to a minimum. Josh looked up and noticed the T.R.I.G.O.M. probes to the left of the pyramid's peak. This was unusual and they crouched down to observe. "They must have some idea that we are here. This is not going to be quite as easy as we thought," Josh whispered to her.

She nodded. "We will have to go as deep as possible to avoid detection. Surely they don't know that we are here!"

They got up slowly and approached the edge of the water, the cool water covering their toes as they slowly walked forward. Torri turned to Josh and pressed the small keypad on the side of his belt. She had explained how to activate the force field and what to do if he experienced any difficulties. Once she had activated the belt, all he felt was a gentle breeze surround his body, everything else was completely normal. She smiled at him. "It does feel a little strange at first when you get below the water, but just swim, talk and move normally."

He nodded, she smiled. They both activated their belts and walked further into the water.

"Just breathe as we go under. You may want to hold your breath, which is a natural instinct but once you relax and breathe, you will be OK." Again he nodded to her that he understood. "You can talk, it's OK. We are linked and we will be able to hear each other clearly." She was trying not to laugh.

"Oh yes sorry, it just feels a little strange." He looked at her amused face and laughed.

"You will still be able to feel and touch. The force field is invisible and allows full interaction."

The water was now up to their waists. Josh looked at Torri. "We must get going quickly to avoid any detection."

She nodded and he squeezed her hand before they headed below the surface of the water.

The storm had worsened and the sky had begun to darken, reducing the light even more. Faint strips of red seemed to mingle with the blackness, casting an eerie light as the lightning flashed overhead and the thunder rumbled in the distance. The world was experiencing savage storms but the majority of the population were completely oblivious, happy in their Avatar worlds. Only a few sensed the danger or the changes around them.

Chapter Thirty-One

After the devastations which had occurred some 20 years ago when the world's climate changed so dramatically, the science which had predicted such change was now no more. Those who had been previously charged to monitor the universe and were given the resources to do so had now been consumed by the urgency to create a new technical age. They were more concerned with the fast developing world of fantasies rather than facing future realities of any degree. The consensus of feeling had been, after these changes, that this was the fulfilment of the "great disaster" which had been predicated long ago; humans had survived and adapted so all would be well. Interest in factual events grew less and any curiosity for the universe or the cosmos were discouraged. This had led to even more human individuality being devoured by T.R.I.G.O.M.

Over this time, planet positions had been slowly changing, including that of the Earth and its orbit around its star. Extremes of weather were now accepted as normal which meant that they had ceased to be monitored or even regarded as important. Ironically, since the beginning of early records, the universe, which had always held a fascination for mankind, which arguably gave birth to religions, inspiring speculations of how our world had been formed and of other life beyond our own solar system, was no more. That once strong human instinct to discover and learn, enabling human evolution and dominance of the creatures of the Earth had gradually been deprogrammed from modern culture. Total dependence lay on T.R.I.G.O.M. to nurture and protect the world's inhabitants and nothing was ever questioned. This was justified by those of the council as freeing the human population to exercise their dreams and desires by virtual means and encountering no danger in doing so. As humans grew less and less curious however, a section of the council overseeing security had become just the opposite and the head of this was Braedan himself.

Braedan had realised that changes were taking place and even with all the vast knowledge that he had access to, they were not fully explainable through any known quantum physics or mathematical formula he knew; it was like another force was in place. He was aware of ancient predictions and beliefs of new worlds yet to come. He had all the data on historical writings of old civilisations, the druids and their magical rituals but artificial life forms could only theorise with hard facts and figures, they were not creative, unlike the human mind and perhaps most fundamentally the human capacity to have faith where no factual evidence exists. Braedan knew something was changing, not climatically, but something he couldn't explain and he was convinced that Patrick would give him the answers. They had just been doing the usual routine checks on visitors coming in to Atbara, when Braedan had recognised Patrick and had made sure that they had picked him to check. It was easy to justify, Patrick and his friend were not the usual visitors they received, they liked the outdoors and something not encouraged by T.R.I.G.O.M. It was not against any laws or protocols so unless any breach of security could be proven they were just monitored periodically to make sure that they were not creating trouble or unrest. The data missing from Patrick's chip gave him the ideal excuse to bring him in for questioning.

Chapter Thirty-Two

Braedan had been watching Patrick for many years and subsequently Joshua because of his close friendship with Patrick. They had no knowledge of this of course as Braedan had done this secretly but anyone that they associated with would also come under his observations.

His interest had started with Patrick many years ago, before Braedan had become what he was today. He only possessed a few human memories which he had tried to hold on to even though it had been many years ago since he had been fully human. Watching Patrick looking so helpless, he started to draw on those few memories. He had never been able to recall much and it seemed that the memories he had were only ever the negative ones involving Patrick. Perhaps that was why he had become obsessed with him and also his own sister Megan, who he could remember had never had time for him or he her. He had been jealous of the love and attention that his parents paid her. He had hated her ability to make friends when he could not remember having a friend at all. He had resented any friendships that she formed and would do whatever he could to discourage or go out of his way to deliberately cause trouble. However, when she developed a friendship with a boy from another part of the world, his usual jealousy had grown more intense but it had also aroused his curiosity. The different lilt in the boy's voice as he spoke, his outgoing personality and his passion for relics fascinated him. They had met briefly, Patrick introducing himself in his usual friendly robust manner but not paying too much attention to this quite sulky-looking boy, who appeared unfriendly and introvert, not like his sister. Patrick's feelings towards Megan had grown in the short time that he had known her but being so young he had not known how to express his feelings to her. He had found that giving her little presents helped him express his boyish love and it made him feel happy. One of these gifts was an old almanac, given to him by his grandfather. Patrick gave it to her with such love and pride, telling her how he had always treasured it and hoped that she would like it. He told her all about his grandfather and the time that they had together. Patrick knew this old almanac contained some articles which were frowned upon by T.R.I.G.O.M. and perhaps it was risky giving it to her, but his infatuation with her was such that nothing else seemed to matter. He had kept it safe and it never occurred to him for a second that she would not do the same. She had readily accepted it, flattered by his attentions but too young to really appreciate the relevance of this gift. As soon as Patrick had gone and after flicking through it and finding it of no interest, she casually dropped it in the waste area. She was young and carefree, heavily spoilt by her parents, not realising the hurt she could cause by her sometimes blasé attitude to life. Braedan had been watching his sister and Patrick, fascinated with Patrick's obvious feelings for his sister. When Megan had disappeared from view he had retrieved the almanac, carefully lifting it from the waste area, stroking it with his fingers as if he had found a pot of gold. The glossy front cover fascinated him as it was like nothing he had seen before, so colourful and bright, not like the colours of the computer generated visuals of the day. He took it to the safety of his room, carefully hiding it away; it was his now. Much later that day, he had gone to his room, making sure that he shut the door behind him; he wanted to look at his new treasure. He took it out from its hiding place and he began to slowly flick through the pages, something which became a daily ritual. He read it from cover to cover. Although it was in very good condition for its age, published in 2030, on closer look he could see that the colours were beginning to fade where the pages had been turned so many times. He felt the delicacy of the paper to his touch and unlike his sister appreciated it as something special. He instinctively knew that this was a rare find and his curiosity grew as he turned each page. Now he was feeling very pleased with himself and started to smile, something he rarely did. If only he had known then what he knew now, perhaps things would have turned out differently.

Chapter Thirty-Three

Joshua tried to breathe normally as they submerged under the water, half expecting to suffocate when he tried to take his first breath, but it was just like breathing fresh air. Once his initial panic had subsided, he relaxed a little, breathing steadily. He looked around and was surprised to see how clear the water was. He had expected it to be murky but he could see small fish, busy darting out of their way. The pyramid itself was not too far away and he looked over at Torri. She was swimming surprisingly well as after all it was a physical activity and she could not have much time for exercise. He knew he would have to pace himself so that he did not become overly tired. Although he had tried to exercise as much as possible with subtle things like walking instead of taking a car, his stamina would not compare to an average person of decades ago, when manual work and strength was a vital part of survival and culture.

They swam slowly towards the pyramid base, Torri had the tool pouch attached to her belt and he had the container ready and waiting. A large eel-like creature swam directly in front of them, looking at them with curiosity but quickly swam off when Torri put her hand out towards it. It was rare to see any marine life these days and Josh found it fascinating but sadly the urgency of their task had taken the edge of fully appreciating this new experience. They were quite deep underwater now but they could see lights above them. Josh nudged Torri and pointed upwards, without speaking. She nodded and pointed downwards, indicating that they should go deeper to avoid any detection from the T.R.I.G.O.M. air probes. They swam downwards; Josh felt something touch his hand. Startled, he began to panic; Torri took his hand. "It's OK. It's just that eel being inquisitive, just breathe slowly."

He took a few deep breaths, trying to squash this feeling of claustrophobia that was beginning to creep over him. They carried on swimming downwards until Torri stopped. "We are deep enough, to go any further could compromise the force field, but we should be alright now and well out of their detection range. Working for T.R.I.G.O.M. does have its uses, knowing its limits may come in useful." She spoke softly but Josh could tell that she was now getting more worried as they neared the pyramid. They both remained quiet, conserving their energy to swim in order to reach their destination.

Decades ago, people would come from all over to visit these great wonders of Egypt but so many things had changed with the world. Even if anyone had become interested they would have soon been put off because it took too much effort to get to, being surrounded by water rather than desert sand. If anyone was even remotely interested in any of the great wonders of the past, they would satisfy their interest only with computer images or within their own Avatar world where no physical energy was required.

As they got closer to the Great Pyramid, the water was much shallower and it was at this point that they both began to feel uneasy. Now that they were coming further to the surface it was increasing their chances of being detected by the overhead probes. Josh pointed to the side of the pyramid where the stone sat that they required. It was just over the opposite side to where they were and they would have to swim around to it. Just then, one of the probes circling the pyramid stopped just above them and they both froze, hardly daring to breathe. At this point they were still below the water but having to kneel on the sandy floor to ensure that their head and shoulders could not be seen from above. Torri put her finger to her lips so that Josh would not say a word, he understood and they both remained silent. Torri had her head tilted upwards so that she could see the probe which had now started to emanate a yellow light, it was searching for something, but she recognised it as a "B" class probe and was not able to detect through water although it could certainly pick up movement. Thankfully, the eel-like creature that they had encountered suddenly appeared, its body just skimming the surface of the water. This was enough distraction for the probe; it turned in the direction of the creature who was heading in the opposite direction from them. The probe followed it for a short time until it had analysed the creature and was satisfied that it was of no interest. Josh gave out a long sigh of relief. "That was lucky. What are those probes doing here? Obviously there is something of great importance here."

Torri nodded her head. "Yes it would seem that way, but perhaps they are not sure what or why. In fact nor are we, but one thing is for sure, we must get to this stone and find out quickly." They stood up and their heads and shoulders pushed upwards to above the water level. Josh was expecting his head to be wet, but he was completely dry, being protected by the force field generated by his underwater belt. They swam towards the other side of the pyramid, their heads above the water, getting slightly deeper as they moved around it. They drew nearer, constantly scanning for any probes but Josh couldn't get rid of the feeling that something was watching them but all appeared to be clear for the moment. It was then he noticed that the eel had returned and it had started circling around them, its shiny skin skimming the surface of the water.

"Look," he said to Torri pointing towards the eel, "our friend has returned, do you think it is looking after us?"

Torri looked in surprise towards it and as she did so, it swam directly towards her. It stopped within a few inches from her face, so near she could see it quite clearly. She looked at it without fear and as she looked at its eyes, she could have sworn that she could hear Evia telling her to hurry. As she stared at it more closely its facial features became distorted, changing. Then she gasped. It reminded her of another creature, yes, it looked like an owl. "Ollie." She shook her head in disbelief.

"You OK?" Josh asked looking over at her a little worried.

"Yes, fine, just my eyes and ears playing tricks on me; I must have some water in them. But, hey, let's hurry up and get this done." The stone was in sight, just an arm's length away.

Chapter Thirty-Four

A sudden jolt brought Braedan out of his thoughts. It had been a small earthquake, nothing out of the ordinary these days but enough to shake the room and disturb his recollections of Patrick and Megan.

Through his observations of Patrick, he was aware of the coffee booth that Joshua and Patrick had visited and had become curious as he could find no information on the old woman in the coffee booth that he had seen in Patrick's thoughts. In fact his records showed just a standard un-manned coffee booth. This oddity needed to be investigated and could be classed a security alert. He would normally send out his Hubots to investigate, however this was more personal and he was intrigued. At first he had decided to wait to see if this woman materialised but his patience had not lasted long and he had become very frustrated with her lack of activity. The probes were failing to provide any information; this old woman seemed able to elude them and he wanted to find out how and learn more about her. It was not very often he left the safety of the T.R.I.G.O.M. headquarters but he decided to visit this coffee booth in person. It was registered as an un-manned booth but none of the sensors had picked up any strange activity and so he needed to know what was happening within it; find this mysterious woman whom he had every intention of arresting. Confident that Patrick was well secured and there would be no risk of his escape, he summoned his transport and armed guard. The T.R.I.G.O.M. council who developed all protocols and monitored all technology, were seemingly unaware of the extent of Braedan's power and resources. He smiled to himself thinking, beware of what you create …

It took less than a few minutes to reach the coffee booth in one of his personal use Air Discs which landed effortlessly beside the booth. There didn't seem to be anything out of the ordinary from the outside just a normal standard coffee booth. Escorted by his Hubots, he entered the booth and observed, his eyes quickly scanning everywhere for any anomalies. It looked exactly as it should, fully automated and the hum of the machinery eased his troubled thoughts. Satisfied that there was nothing untoward, he sent his Hubots back to the Air Disc; he wanted to stay for a while. He sat down alone at one of the vacant tables, in an effort to understand the love for these places and this drink called Coffee which he found disgusting. However, it had been some time since he had last tasted it and so he requested a cup. It promptly arrived and he took a sip, after all he wanted to appear normal to enable him to observe with the hope that he may be able to entice this woman to appear. As he sat, taking another sip of coffee, he found that he started to recall back again to his first meeting with Patrick and his recollections of his sister. He had only been able to remember back to the point of that almanac, it was blank after that but he felt very strongly that this was when his hatred and obsession with Patrick started. He sipped the coffee again, its taste bitter at first but after a while it became more palatable which surprised him. This coffee booth was having a strange effect on him; his thoughts became clearer, his mind transporting back in time, and he was a boy again, opening that almanac for the first time in the safety of his bedroom. He had soon realised that this was no ordinary almanac, it had all manner of information contained within it. A section about Edgar Cayce in the late 1800s to early 1900s and his belief in a new age, combining all religions and spiritual realms making up a new world; pseudoscience; the writings of Aristotle, Plato and other ancient philosophers. There was one section suggesting that there was a secret Hall of Records hidden beneath the Sphinx; he remembered how enthralled he had felt reading its contents. What most fascinated him were the astrological predictions contained within it and he realised that most of these predictions had actually happened. His interest grew. This almanac had just been re-styled from the old almanacs of the very early years but had managed to condense only the true events of the past with alarming predictions for the future which did not include T.R.I.G.O.M. He recalled that he had tried to look up information on the T.R.I.G.O.M. information system but had found nothing available. The exact predictions he had found in the almanac he could not recall, they seemed to have been erased from his mind but he could now actually remember how he had felt after reading them, alarmed and frightened with a sickness in his stomach. It had been so long since he had experienced strong emotional feelings that he had to hold on to the small coffee table to stabilise himself as the booth seemed to be spinning. What was happening to him here? He steadied himself, his mind again focusing on the past. He remembered his sister bursting into his bedroom, accompanied by their parents, his sister shouting, "Look I told you he had it." She looked at him with such fury and in an instant he had realised that her jealousy of him was far greater than his of her. All the times that he had caused trouble for her, instigating the loss of her friends. All these things overwhelmed her and he could see that look of revenge in her eyes and for the first time he felt afraid. His parents had been appalled at this find and had quickly confiscated the almanac, locked him in his room and told him that they would deal with him later. He had been shocked at this outburst, not quite understanding what had just happened. Confused, he had sobbed for what seemed an eternity, alone in his room. The loneliness he felt overwhelmed him; he sobbed as though his heart was breaking, inwardly crying out for love and acceptance, something that his parents never gave him. That was all that he had needed, love. Braedan was overwhelmed by these memories which he had forgotten or that had deliberately been erased from his mind and now he saw more …

His parents were high in the ranking order within the protocol section of T.R.I.G.O.M. and had felt it their duty to report their son to the board and hand in this almanac which contained unfavourable material. They had not even questioned Braedan as to its origin and why he had it in his possession. Megan was in her element at first but then her smug smile ceased; she had not thought that he would get into so much trouble. She had seen Braedan take the almanac from the waste area and had observed him looking at the pages, looking so pleased with himself. Although she was younger than him, she was very intelligent and had a better understanding of people and behaviour than he had. She had soon realised that the book contained unfavourable material, perhaps this was an opportunity to get him into a little trouble, a little pay back after all the trouble that he had created for her. He had never had time for her, always cold towards her and found every opportunity to get her into trouble. She had craved his attention when she had been much younger, only to be continually rejected by him, so she thought it would be fun to reverse the roles. She had seen no need to mention Patrick and had told her parents that she had seen Braedan with the book and heard him telling people of its contents, promoting curiosity within areas which were taboo. She had not realised the gravity of her accusations and to what cost. She was not a malicious person by nature and had genuinely been shaken as to the extent of the trouble she had got Braedan into. It was not long after this that Braedan had been taken away, his parents watching quietly, their heads lowered as he had been taken away to the Red Zone … He was shaking at the recollection, it was then he felt a hand on his shoulder, he turned quickly and Evia was facing him.

Chapter Thirty-Five

"Patrick, wake up." He thought he heard a soft voice in the distance. The blackness in front of his eyes was being replaced with light and then very gradually he opened his eyes. He seemed to be completely submerged in a blue liquid but surprisingly he could breathe. He felt panic engulfing his body, his brain telling him he should be drowning but the reality was different. He vaguely remembered the containers, which looked like large test tubes that he had passed when he was being taken to the Red Zone. Was this where he was? His eyes now began to focus but he couldn't move, he didn't seem to be in control of his body. The only thing he could move was his eyes. He tried to look around him, the liquid making his vision blurred. He could just make out that right next to him was another container but this one had a reddish glow and had something dark inside it. Just then a Hubot walked past him, suddenly stopping. He shut his eyes instinctively but he knew it was lingering outside his tube. He could feel his heart beginning to race. The Hubot spoke to him. "You are now connected to us all, we sense you as you sense us, you can open your eyes." Patrick opened his eyes, the Hubot was looking straight at him. Its eyes seemed to be a piercing blue. He had seen those eyes before. The Hubot continued. "You will soon be part of T.R.I.G.O.M. ready to contribute to our growth and evolution."

Patrick could not speak but as he thought the words, the computer spoke them. "I do not want to be a part of T.R.I.G.O.M. What right do you have to do this?"

The Hubot, having a partial human face, seemed to smile but those piercing eyes, still cold and emotionless, made Patrick feel even colder than he already was. "Don't worry, Patrick, it won't be long and then you will embrace your new self." It turned and walked away, leaving him alone, helpless and lost. He closed his eyes again, hoping that it was just a terrible dream and he would wake up back at the hotel room waiting for Josh to return. He heard that soft voice again, so faint but he was sure he wasn't imagining it. "P a t r i c k , do not be afraid, we are here to help you." He could barely make out the words but he felt suddenly comforted. "They will not be able to hear us. We are here but in a different vibration to the normal physical existence and they cannot penetrate our force." It was then that he recognised the voice as that of the old man he had met at the caves, Admar and there was another voice which sounded feminine but it was hard to distinguish as they seemed to speak together as one voice. He mentally shouted for help. The voices answered him. "Do not think to speak, please just listen. They cannot hear us but they can hear you and although we can block out most things, because you are attached to T.R.I.G.O.M. it makes things more difficult." Patrick tried to control this surge of panic that he could feel welling up through his whole being. "We will come for you shortly. Please try not to be frightened, but we will get you out of here and into safety, you have done your job well and kept the charm safe all these years but you are not finished yet." The voices had gone and silence engulfed him again, he hadn't understood but he had begun to feel calmer. Whilst they had been talking to him, there had been a constant sound of humming around him and it was only when the voices had stopped that he had realised how loud it had been.

Suddenly a Hubot appeared in front of him and as he looked closer, he realised that the Hubot had those same piercing eyes as Braedan. Was Braedan human or something else? "We seemed to have lost you for a few moments there, which wasn't supposed to happen." It was looking at him, Patrick could feel that it was full of suspicion and yes, even hatred. Patrick couldn't tell this from its blank expression but he knew that it was there. The Hubot had been right in that he did feel somehow connected to them but only in the sense of their thoughts, nothing more. He looked at the Hubot, knowing that the computer would speak as he thought. "What are you doing to me and why?" The Hubot showed no emotion at all and Patrick could sense its coldness again. It did not reply and he could sense nothing more; he was not fully integrated with them yet.

Suddenly the Hubot backed away from Patrick; it seemed to have received some information which took away his attention. Patrick did not hear what was said but he could almost feel the alarm. "Quick before it is too late." He didn't understand what that meant but Joshua came quickly into his thoughts. His understanding of technology was not the greatest by modern standards, but he wondered, as he was actually connected to T.R.I.G.O.M. then perhaps he could have some sort of influence on its actions or at least find out what was happening. He decided to concentrate and see what, if anything came to his thoughts. He closed his eyes and at first could only see a blue mist, just like the liquid he was submerged in, but then it got brighter; a paler colour. He tried to clear his mind using an old meditation technique he had learned as a young boy. He felt a sharp pain in his head as what seemed to be a thousand voices all speaking together, exploded into his brain making him want to cry out with the intensity of it. He felt such loss, pain and deep sorrow, he couldn't bear it and the pain in his head was intensifying. "Concentrate," he thought to himself trying to calm himself. He needed to find out if he could help Josh. He concentrated harder, the voices were becoming clearer. "Help us, we are trapped, they have taken away our flesh and we are locked in these machines."

Then some other voice. "They are at the Great Pyramid, we must get there."

"Help us, help us." A multitude of voices overwhelmed him again as he tried to meditate, the pain engulfing his body until he wanted to scream. He could take no more.

Just as he thought he was going to pass out again, his whole body felt light as if he was floating upwards. His brain told him that his body was still submerged in the tube. Were his meditation skills better than he had thought? No, he knew that it was something else; he could feel another energy. He was rising upwards as he started to focus and began to see clearly as he looked down. He gasped at what he saw. He was looking at his body lying so still in the blue liquid which held it captive. It looked emotionless and cold but he felt alive and free. Quickly, he looked around and there was Admar looking straight at him and holding out his hand. "We have no time to lose, don't worry, your body is safe in the tube for now. They will think that you are dead, don't worry I will explain." Patrick was not frightened and he just knew that now he was safe …

Chapter Thirty-Six

Joshua pointed to the stone, but just then a T.R.I.G.O.M. security drone which had taken over from the usual probe was heading straight at them. Torri looked at Josh in panic. "They have seen us, they know we are here." The drone was pulsating creating a red hue and was heading their way. "Josh," she shouted, "quick, we must dive for the stone." And they submerged, not stopping until the stone was in front of them. The drone had penetrated the water, they looked at each other in panic. It must be the highly advanced security model, the usual drones stayed airborne at all times and they both knew that it would use force if it was deemed necessary.

Torri got to the stone first and as she touched the stone she noticed that her bracelet, which was still firmly attached to her wrist, began to glow. Josh had also noticed the bracelet; its glow and warmth seemed to emanate through the water. At first the stone just looked like the others, maybe slightly larger but nothing special. The old stones of the pyramid were decaying badly now and the water had certainly taken its toll over recent decades. From the moment that Torri touched the stone, the dust started to disappear. It just seemed to fall away in front of her and what once looked like old sand dust, slowly disappeared, revealing a shiny sort of metal.

"Look," Josh shouted in amazement, "it's just like the drawings that we saw."

He didn't have time to say any more as suddenly the probe was in front of them. "You will come with me now." It spoke without emotion. "You have broken security parameters and are requested back at T.R.I.G.O.M. headquarters." Even though they were all fully submerged, they heard very clearly. It seemed to have some sort of weapon which Josh did not recognise but knew that it would not hesitate to use force if its request was not complied with. Josh edged his way in front of Torri, in direct line with the drone. Torri quickly turned towards the stone. She knew she had to keep her hand on it and then felt a compulsion to take Josh's hand. As Torri grabbed Josh's hand, he felt a sharp burning pain in his arm, exactly where the symbol-like tattoo had appeared on his skin. The pain was so sharp that he nearly passed out. Torri held his hand tighter. Another rush of searing pain and then the tattoo vanished from his arm. Torri gasped as she saw the symbols appear on the metal slab. A ring of bright light surrounded them both as the drone charged its weapon. As it fired, the laser of energy it generated to harm them, rebounded back to the drone and in a split second it had been completely destroyed.

Josh looked at Torri with utter astonishment as the drone disintegrated before their eyes, the ring of light shielding them against any impact from the aftermath of the drone's destruction. Their bodies were not even swaying as the water swirled angrily around them. The blast caused the waves on the surface to rise and crash down, but they remained protected and unharmed. As the waters calmed, the ring of light began to fade and as quickly as it had appeared it was gone. Torri let go of Josh's hand; she was drawn to the stone on the pyramid. As she looked she realised that it now shone brightly, lighting up her face as she stood transfixed, unable to divert her eyes from its metallic glow. It was only Josh's sudden gasp of pain that jolted her from her trance-like state. A sharp pain in his arm had made Josh cry out and grab it. He inspected his arm where the tattoo-like symbols had been. Incredibly he had no scars or damaged tissue; it was if they had never been there. The pain in his arm quickly abated. He had no more pain, for the first time in a long time. He gently stroked his skin where it had been, it felt soft to the touch. The only thing different was that it was devoid of any bodily hair and very smooth. He looked up at the metallic looking slab and he marvelled at the symbols which had once been embedded, sometimes painfully, in his arm, they were shining brightly on the smooth metal slab. Torri too, looked at them in amazement and then gently touched his arm, as if for reassurance that he was alright. She instinctively looked down at her bracelet and although it was still firmly on her wrist, it had begun to glow as brightly as the metal slab in front of her. Both of them were silent, caught up in events which seemed to be out of their control, the air around them charged with a magical aura and they both felt tingles of excitement running through their bodies. It was like time had stood still. They could hear crackles of energy as light flickered around the pyramid; they dared not move. They were both drawn instantaneously to look down at the bracelet as it had begun to visibly pulsate, emanating a soft humming noise which broke into the dead silence which had precluded. Torri's wrist began to feel warm but not uncomfortable and as one of the symbols began to glow brighter than the rest, she felt a sudden urge to touch it. As her fingers touched the symbol she felt a slight tingle as it disappeared from the bracelet and lit up the corresponding symbol on the metallic slab before them, at the same time giving off a perfect musical note of such incredible clarity. She gasped as this happened and Josh jumped back a little. She felt no fear as she looked again at the bracelet. The second symbol had now begun to glow brighter within the charm hanging from the bracelet. Once again she touched it with her finger. The symbol disappeared and lit up the metal slab as before. Josh looked at her in amazement. There were six symbols in the charm. They both looked again now expecting the next symbol to glow and they were not disappointed. This continued until they got to the sixth symbol. Josh looked at her; they both knew what the other was thinking but they dared not speak. What was going to happen when the last symbol reached the metal? They both wanted to speak but the air around them seemed so charged with electricity, they felt that if they spoke it would break this magic spell which had been woven around them. As each symbol had been transferred, a beautiful musical note enchanted the air with its sound and got louder with each symbol. Although it was a loud sound it was also exquisite, enchanting and was accompanied with a strong vibration which they could physically feel; starting at their feet and working upwards through their bodies. Just then the eel-like creature they had seen before, swam past them, flicking its tail frantically. Torri instinctively knew that this was a sign to hurry. She looked at Josh, unafraid, smiling as her fingers reached for the sixth symbol. It was then they both noticed in horror that there was a place for a seventh symbol and yet the bracelet only had six.

Chapter Thirty-Seven

The coffee booth had changed around him which he hadn't noticed at first. The minimalistic modern décor of the usual unmanned coffee booths had disappeared giving way to an old fashioned American diner. He wondered if he had time travelled or was still recalling memories but then he looked up and there she was before him, Braedan stared coldly at her. There was no need for introduction, she sat down opposite him.

"You know who I am." Braedan broke the silence.

"I do know who you are but do you really know who you are?" She answered him with a question. He looked puzzled, there was no sign of fear in her face, something which he was not used to seeing from people he spoke to in the manner that he just had. She was so calm and not undermined in the slightest by his presence or his demeanour. She did not wait for him to answer but continued. "Here you will remember who you really are." Normally he would have called for his guards but his subconscious curiosity for his past life which he had not been able to recall stopped him.

"What do you mean?" Before he could move, she placed the palm of her hand on his forehead. He could feel all the artificial parts of his body, they were heavy and felt like they were stopping, being replaced with something else, perhaps his lost humanity. He continued to remember as if he were a third party observing …

He had been swiftly taken away to the Red Zone, ironically the place he would one day control. He had not seen his parents or sister again for a long time but later, he had made sure that he repaid them for their actions. He had been a frightened young boy, feeling totally abandoned by everyone and having no clue what was about to happen to him. The uniformed officers escorting him away looked big and menacing, no kind words of comfort, just cold and silent. He didn't know if they were human or Android; Androids being the most advanced artificial life form back then. He was not used to the outdoors and everywhere looked scary and unfamiliar. He wanted to cry but he was frozen with terror and the tears would not flow. He hadn't realised that by possessing this almanac it would cause so much trouble. He hated his sister, his parents and he hated Patrick. After all it was his almanac; it was his fault that this was happening. Braedan was young but like his sister, he was very intelligent, standing out in his studies to the point where he had been noticed by the council. As his terror started to ease or was he just getting used to the situation, it suddenly occurred to him that no one had even questioned him about anything. "Curious," he thought. He hadn't even been given the opportunity of explaining or telling anyone about Patrick and his sister. This made him wonder if there was an ulterior motive as to why he was being brought to T.R.I.G.O.M. The latter proved to be correct.

There was a section of the council, not widely supported, who were determined to advance artificial intelligence further. They were convinced that they could join a human and an artificial life form together, not to create but rather to give birth to a sanctioned being; the first of a kind. However the main council body would not approve the ethics when detailed experiments were presented to them and human sacrifice could not be accepted. Although it had been declined the supporters of this experiment did not put it to rest and largely acted in secret. They were constantly looking for the right candidate and the right opportunity to conduct their experiments. Braedan had been brought to their attention through his constantly outstanding study record but he was also a loner and did not make friends easily. This suited their purpose and the other bonus was that his parents worked for T.R.I.G.O.M. and could be easily manipulated. Their decision to inform on their son regarding his dubious reading material could not have come at a better time and one which could not have been planned. It was the perfect excuse to detain the boy, the reason for his detention was of no real interest to the council, they did not take great interest in old magazines, but it served their purpose and no questions would be asked.

Braedan did not have long to theorise before his fate claimed him. He was taken to a small clinical room where he was securely detained. He shouted out for his mum; no one heard his cries. His kicking and struggling were to no avail, he had been abandoned by all those close to him. These were his last memories, fiercely engulfing his whole being; abandonment, loss and even hate all etched into his soul. Then, after he could struggle no more, his energy leaving him as his despair enfolded him, he was finally sedated. He lost consciousness, his small frail body limp as he was completely submerged in a specially prepared preserving tube, waiting for his creator, the boy lost forever.

Chapter Thirty-Eight

It had been easy to keep Braedan's rebirth secret from the human sector of T.R.I.G.O.M. His human brain modified and combined with an entity which had secretly been evolved by the mainframe computer, with unsuspecting assistance from its human benefactors. Nanobots inside the computer had developed an embryo sack, full of a rich substance similar to the primeval soup which gave birth to the first known life forms. Each Nanobot specifically programmed with its own DNA to create working and living organs ready to adapt to any environment. His intellect transferred via an umbilical cord of fine silvery fibre optics, combining artificial and human together so that his intelligence would be unequalled by any one form of life; a built in thirst for knowledge and a need to understand giving drive to this being. However, the human essence which still had never been defined was not fully captivated within this experiment and so it had not been graded as completely successful. With all his superhuman intelligence he lost many human attributes. He was fully aware of this, as he knew he was different from everyone else but was it something he could re-learn? He needed to know. He was not however, devoid of all emotion. It seemed that he could fully experience negative emotions; rage, when things didn't go his way and jealousy. He was jealous of human love and compassion which he often witnessed, leaving questions in his mind; was he indeed the answer to higher advancement? Could it be that it was not knowledge but the capacity to love that was more important? It was this question that drove him into terrible fits of rage when he could find no solid answers. He was the first and only one of his kind, but he had lost human emotion and could not find faith in anything that was not scientific. He no longer possessed the human capacity for abstract thinking, he only understood logic. He would always remain the only one as further experiments had been shelved; there would not be another Braedan. He was alone with no one to relate to and although perhaps loneliness was not what he felt, he had a sense of something missing from his existence but didn't know quite what it was. He was compelled by a need to learn and experience that which was human. Ironically he had been created as a higher form of intelligent life to enhance the evolution of the planet but instead strived for the fundamental feelings of these lesser intelligent beings of which he had once been.

He felt Evia's hand on his shoulder again but this time he felt her love. He was that small boy again; he wanted to cry.

"It was never your fault." She spoke softly but he sobbed now.

"You don't know the things that I have done."

She nodded her head. "I know everything that you have done. You tried to kill Joshua, you tried to hurt Patrick. You had your parents and sister taken for experimental purposes. You were not totally responsible for your actions but there is a part of you that was."

"What have you done to me?"

"Nothing that will not revert back as soon as you leave, but I wanted you to know the truth and why you are as you are now. You will never be totally lost and one day you will be the person you once were." She looked at him with sadness. "Your bitterness and jealousy will not help you now, but you must help prepare for the change. You cannot stop the future, it is destined, but you have a purpose here and now to ease the suffering that is about to descend upon you. When you leave this protected place, you will become as you were but you will remember and I only hope that this will help you in the things that are to come."

"Who are you? How do you have such power?" he asked incredulously.

She smiled. "I have been known as many names throughout your history." She said nothing more and then he watched as she just disappeared in front of his eyes. The room became brighter; he hadn't realised how still everything had become when Evia had appeared. Now he could feel his body coming back to life; it felt heavy. He was again the Artificial Life Form known as Braedan.

Chapter Thirty-Nine

Admar looked at Patrick and smiled. Evia had joined them at this point. As Patrick looked at her he noticed that she glowed, her body was outlined with a soft white light, and her face had all her features, not of flesh but of light. He held out his arms in front of him to inspect his hands, every feature accentuated by the same light. He could move so fast, seemingly without effort and felt so alive and full of energy. He knew that he was in a natural form of light and anything he thought about he knew the answers and understood instantly. His knowledge seemed limitless; quantum mechanics, the theories of which he had never understood before; the possibilities of being in two places at the same time; secrets of the universe. It was wonderful, he understood everything. His body was not physical but Admar had told him this condition would not last long. He would be returning to his physical form and he would not remember this knowledge he had been allowed to have and experience for a short time. It had been necessary to get him out of the tube. They had to make T.R.I.G.O.M. believe he was dead but in reality he was just in a different vibration, a different level of existence. He was indeed being given the privilege of this experience which would sadly not last. The power of thought alone could convey words within a second, no sound or movement of lips required. He felt euphoric with a strong sense of being home which gave him a safe and familiar feeling. Patrick saw the Earth in its entirety, as storms were building and growing stronger all over the globe. Flashes of lightning so bright that they could be seen past the hemisphere; Patrick could see it all. The tectonic plates underneath the Earth's surface had increased in their activity as the Earth's orbit continued in its change, the gravitational pull of the moon slowly losing its hold. The moon had taken on a reddish glow which had gone un- noticed by most of the Earth's population.

They carried on in their own worlds of fantasy and those few who did observe took no real interest. Patrick's feelings of anxiety for the Earth and mankind only briefly held his thoughts and instead he was overwhelmed by his feelings of elation and hope, knowing the possibilities for the future. He watched as a giant tidal wave started to pick up momentum on the South American coast of Florida. He saw the rivers created by the Iguassu Falls start to bubble as a large crack below the Earth's crust, created by the movements of tectonic plates, had forced hot magma closer to the surface. Winds of incredible force which had never been experienced before had begun to spread across the globe. Soon it would be hard to ignore and even those lost in their fantasy worlds would not be able to escape reality. As Patrick looked to the Earth's star, the Sun, he saw its colour starting to change. It was getting darker, its redness dimming and its warmth lessening as the Earth continued to change position within the planetary system, Jupiter's moon Europa breaking away from its giant guardian and heading for its new destination as Mercury headed ever closer to the Sun for its rebirth into solar energy. Patrick could not physically feel the effects of these changes, but could experience it through an extra sense which left him without discomfort or fear. He could hear the rumbles of thunder which came from the continents remaining on the Earth. The lightning which struck and destroyed all that it contacted, was fast spreading and setting the dryer areas alight with fires raging out of control. He knew now that he must look to Torri and Josh to make sure that all was as it should be.

Chapter Forty

The Hubot looked at Patrick's body, suspended in his tube and then looked closer. It realised now that his body was lifeless and no signals were coming from his brain. It was impossible. He couldn't have … died. The Hubot hardly dare form the thought in its mind. The computer had been in control of his body, but even though that was the case, he was devoid of life, nothing there but his body, hanging limp and emotionless. The Hubot stared incredulously, unable to understand what had happened, quickly interacting with the main frame computer to try to find an explanation. Even though his body could be used, they had wanted his living brain. Braedan must be informed and quickly, they knew he would be furious but perhaps they had better make sure that Patrick was dead and find out how it had happened. The Hubot initiated the procedure to disconnect the body from its links to T.R.I.G.O.M. and take it out of the tube. They would then dismember it to try and discover the cause of death as nothing was immediately forthcoming. The silvery threads started to disconnect themselves from Patrick's body and the blue fluid started to ebb away. Patrick watched; he was floating in front of the tube, his presence completely undetectable. It was like witnessing a piece of artwork being unthreaded, each strand individually slipping back into the main frame computer and although he could feel no coldness it made him shiver. What had happened to all those innocent people who had been taken into the Red Zone? Some of those people taken had only been guilty of speaking out if they had not agreed with the council's work and their disappearance had helped to ensure that few spoke out for fear that they might meet the same fate.

Patrick could now see his body clearly as the fluid drained away, lying at the bottom of the tube looking completely lifeless. A surgical looking table had been lowered from the ceiling and stopped beside the tube. The Hubots quickly transferred his body on to it, offering no delicacy or respect in their handling of his body as to them he was no more than a piece of meat which they had no need of. The Hubots temporarily left the room and immediately Admar was beside him again. "We must act quickly, we haven't got long. You must concentrate and do as I say without question." Patrick nodded. "You will be transferred back into your body, but you have known what it is like to be free so you will feel uncomfortable initially and you will not retain the vast knowledge that you have now." Again Patrick nodded. He was not sure that he wanted to go back but he knew he must do everything to help Josh and Torri. They needed him and what he knew now, however momentarily, he knew he would possess it again one day. "Once you are back inside your body you will not have long to escape but I will guide you," Admar continued. "Close your eyes and concentrate."

Patrick closed his eyes. He felt drawn to his body, as if he was being pulled by an invisible energy, drawing him down. He felt himself entering his body. The heaviness of it seemed almost unbearable as the blood began to flow through his veins and his heart pumping hurt his chest. His eyes opened. He was so cold he was hardly able to lift up his head from the table he was lying on. There wasn't any time to adjust and it was only through sheer determination that he was able to pull the heavy weight of his body up from the table, only just managing to stop himself falling on to the floor. Admar was in front of him, offering him a drink of the blue liquid that had engulfed his body. "Drink this. It will replace the energy that you have lost and give you strength." Patrick didn't argue he drank the liquid and slowly put on the clothes that Admar provided for him. It was a suit which felt so heavy, covering his whole body including his head. Admar told him he must wear it to avoid detection and that it would make him invisible to any sensors within T.R.I.G.O.M.

Chapter Forty-One

Braedan had returned from the coffee booth, he felt different; the coldness of his artificial form still with him but he now had some of his memories back and he could actually feel the loss of his past identity. No more just an emotionless hybrid of machinery and living tissue, it seemed that something in that coffee booth had changed him, something far more advanced than T.R.I.G.O.M. The compatibility between the human parts of his brain and the artificial parts had been medically successful, but where he gained the understanding of the most complex mathematical equations which he could work out at lightning speed he had lost the human qualities of love and compassion. He had strived to resolve this problem, but this could not be resolved with a mathematical formula so what power did this Evia and this coffee booth have to seemingly solve the impossible? He didn't feel so agitated, he felt quite calm. He was still part of T.R.I.G.O.M. and although he had realised a long time ago they had not much interest in him, just a failed experiment, his mission had always been to learn, preserve and protect at all costs.

Braedan had returned quickly to T.R.I.G.O.M. after he had been informed of Patrick's death and he was now staring at the empty table where Patrick's body had lain. How could he have escaped? The readings had been checked, he had been dead, yet his body had gone and he could not be detected. He knew that the pyramid must be of importance. Did it hold the knowledge that Evia and Admar seemed to have? He had to find out and the only way was to physically go and see for himself. The temperature outside had plummeted to −20 degrees within a matter of hours and was showing no signs of warming up. It would be hard for human or artificial life to function for long periods outside in these extremes; he needed to hurry. The loss of the drone had not sent him into his normal rage. He remained calm, he had come to realise that nothing was impossible and not everything was under the control of T.R.I.G.O.M. He decided that he would go straight to the pyramid to investigate and immediately summoned up one of his fleet of discs. Whilst he was waiting for it to arrive he reflected on the changes that were happening around him, observing from his satellite images. The blue atmosphere which had often been described as a beauty feature of the Earth when observed by early astronauts in their exploration of outer space he now noticed had a reddish hue to it, the red devouring the blue. Braedan's data had revealed that the water levels all over the globe had started to recede, water was evaporating rapidly and the hemisphere was getting weaker as the moon cycle and Earth's orbit changed. This was happening very quickly and his data had also indicated signs that Jupiter, the giant gas planet was getting closer to them, its famous red spot not as prominent as its molecular make up was showing change, its gases rapidly solidifying. It was happening so quickly, the like of which was unprecedented.

Chapter Forty-Two

Patrick followed Admar, his pace getting faster as his energy slowly started to return. Passing tube after tube along the long corridor that seemed never ending, its coldness made Patrick shiver. He remembered the voices asking for help but for now he couldn't stop; he had to get out of this place. Hubots had started coming towards him, their red alert lights flashing. He froze in horror. Admar reassured him. "They can't detect you as the suit makes you invisible to their sensors." It was so strange seeing Hubots passing so close to him, not knowing he was there. Suddenly a Hubot stopped right in front of him, its eyes seemingly looking straight through him. He knew that it couldn't see him but if it touched him he would be detected. He just stopped in time; a few seconds more and they would have collided. For a moment it just hovered there as if waiting for instructions. Patrick dared hardly breathe, turning to one side very slowly to get out of its way and as he turned he realised that he was right in front of one of the tubes. He looked closer. Through the thick substance that filled it, he thought he could see something in there. He drew a sharp breath. It looked like a body submerged in the liquid. The Hubot also turned towards the tube. Patrick began to panic. Perhaps he could be detected after all and Admar was a long way in front of him; he couldn't shout. The Hubot turned to the tube and just stared at it putting out its hand to touch it. Patrick was surprised, the outline of the body inside became clearer. It looked like a young girl. The Hubot put out its other hand and the body inside seemed to be drawn to it. Patrick took a look at the Hubot's face. It was the usual standard issue. The human part of its face looked familiar but he couldn't place it, then he looked again at the body in the tube, its face suddenly hitting the side of the tube making Patrick jump. He knew that face. It was the young girl he had met and fallen in love with all those years ago as a mere boy. "MEGAN." He shouted her name and the Hubot pulled away from the tube and as it did so the dark fluid swallowed up the body again. Patrick knew it had heard him. He stood completely still as it looked around. He could see Admar waving to him to hurry up in the distance. Patrick stepped aside as the Hubot started forward, it was satisfied that no one was there but as it passed him he thought it looked so sad. He must have imagined it.

He hurried to catch up with Admar who led him to the Air Disc platform. "Quickly get inside as Braedan will be here before you know it. He has summoned the disc. He has realised that the pyramid is important, which it is, so hurry. You need to get inside the disc and wait for him. Hide somewhere, it is your lift to the pyramid. Follow your instincts. You will know what to do."

"What about you?" Patrick started to ask but Admar had vanished.

Patrick stepped into the Air Disc and looked around. It was one of the highest graded discs, blue in colour, fully equipped and ready to go. He would have expected no less, after all this was one of a fleet of Air Discs that Braedan had ready at all times for any security issues or urgent business. He looked around for the best place to wait. He had to act quickly, he could hear footsteps.

Chapter Forty-Three

The Air Disc started its initialising sequence ready for its passenger, its destination already programmed. Patrick felt nervous, Braedan would board soon, he didn't really know what he was supposed to do but with everything that had happened to him lately he would not be surprised at anything. The footsteps got louder as Braedan drew closer. Patrick saw the outline of his shape from his hiding place as he watched Braedan enter the disc from his boarding platform, walking straight over to his seat ready for take-off. Patrick shivered as he noticed the line of Hubots along the far side of the disc. They were in stasis mode, always ready and waiting for their command. The blue Air Disc shot straight up from the landing ring and headed towards Giza. Braedan sat looking out through the bubble window looking down at the planet below him; it was changing so fast. He started to ponder. Radical climate changes had happened before but none witnessed like this. It wasn't just climate, the planet was changing position as were the other planets in the solar system. Could this have happened before? Perhaps Mars had once been home to life but had moved from its life giving position within the solar system. Could beings have looked up from Mars, at the other inhospitable planets in the skies? Could one have them been Earth? They had certainly found indicators that life had once existed on Mars and so it had always been open to speculation and theory. Earth may have looked no more than a cold, barren place many millions of years ago. Did it shift position and in doing so evolve to provide life once again? Could another planet do the same thing? Life, death, life continuum. His reflections were interrupted by a shuffling sound coming from behind him. He turned around to investigate. Patrick was in front of him. He had decided to take off his suit in a spur of the moment decision; he was following his instincts. Although he knew that he could have remained there, hidden, for the rest of the journey until they had reached the pyramid, as he had observed Braedan, he had felt a sadness about him that had not been there before and watching him looking out at the Earth below him, Patrick had a gut feeling that it was the right thing to do. Braedan could hardly believe his eyes. "You were supposed to be dead." His voice only a whisper with the shock of what he was seeing. Patrick had no fear now, not even of the Hubots which he knew Braedan could summon to his command at any time. Braedan made no attempt to activate them; his experience at the coffee booth had changed him, he had his memories back. It felt strange, experiencing emotions that he could not remember from before when he had been a boy. He felt emptiness, a longing for something out of his reach; these feelings so strong that they were almost tangible. He suddenly occurred to him that he was feeling loneliness and now seeing Patrick strangely pleased him. He was not a machine or part machine. Here in front of him was a human being whom he had treated so badly but had a past connection to. He needed to feel connected. Patrick had been watching him as he had sat staring out of the window and had sensed this change in him, that unfeeling coldness about him gone. He looked at him, wanting to hate him for what he had done to him but found only pity in his heart. He knew he had to face him.

"As you can see, I'm not dead but very much alive so T.R.I.G.O.M. is not without flaws." Patrick looked straight at him as he spoke. He couldn't help the sharpness in his voice.

"Yes, I can see that, Patrick. You managed to go undetected." Braedan answered in almost a whisper, devoid of his usual authoritative sneer. Patrick pointed to his suit and Braedan nodded understanding the deception.

"Perhaps a product of our mysterious friends Admar and Evia." He smiled. "You may not believe me, Patrick, but I am actually glad that you are not dead."

They both looked at each other in silence, those once blue, piercing eyes had changed to a softer shade, not cold and emotionless like before.

Patrick continued. "Why do you feel so threatened by me and my friend? What is it that you wanted from me?"

Braedan looked at him with sadness. "Do you remember when you were a young boy and you came to Egypt?"

Patrick looked at him puzzled, of course he remembered that time. The face of Megan in that tube flashed before him. It was the first time he had fallen in love and one that he had always remembered. The experience had affected him profoundly.

Braedan didn't give him the chance to reply, he knew that he did. "I was Megan's brother. You would have known me as Michael."

Patrick continued staring at him taking in this revelation. "I took that almanac you gave her. It was amazing; the information it contained was incredible. It told of the past but also the future, a new world so much different to what we have today."

Patrick had read it many times and shared the same passion, often wondering what had happened to it. He had given it to Megan, a token of his great love for her and in the process had not only lost Megan but also his treasured possession. He had wanted to ask for it back after she had laughed at him but could not pluck up the courage to do so. He could not bear to face her again, to look at that beautiful face that he had loved so much and so instead he had taken his damaged ego and broken heart back home. Braedan continued. "It told of a great change to the Earth which would cease to exist as we know it but of a force that would ensure that humanity continues. I read this over and over, enthralled and possessed by boyhood imagination but as you know that sort of material was not looked on favourably by T.R.I.G.O.M. I was found out by my parents and this is my punishment." He pointed to himself. "I blamed you for my fate. If you had not had that almanac I wouldn't be here like this. Megan would have been here, my parents would have been alive and although most of my memories from before had been taken from me, the ones that had caused the most pain had remained. Perhaps punishment from a far greater power than we can know. I realise now that it had nothing to do with the Almanac and that was just an excuse to take me." He had started to get angry but then he looked at Patrick and said softly, "But then the painful memories are created by the most forceful emotions so perhaps that is why I was always able to remember them. In the Almanac, I was glad to take comfort in its words; to imagine that things would change. I desperately wanted a friend like you but you were only interested in Megan. If only I could have spoken to you about those writings, to debate their meanings, that would have meant so much to me but you were only interested in yourself and her."

Patrick drew in a long breath. He now remembered him, Megan's brother. He knew he had tried to talk to him and he was right, his attention had only been with his sister. Perhaps if he had paid him some attention, could he have stopped all this? He wanted to ask him what had happened to Megan and his parents but just then one of the Hubots moved, its light starting to flash. "Quickly," Braedan whispered, "put your suit back on so that they can't see you. I am still part of T.R.I.G.O.M. and my thoughts connected. I have not initialised the Hubot, it would have been done so automatically if a security threat is detected."

Patrick looked at Braedan. "I will put on my suit but please tell me what happened to Megan, I need to know."

Chapter Forty-Four

As Braedan looked at Patrick to speak, his eyes were filled with tears and he related his story in a soft whisper. "Megan was just a girl but unlike most girls of her years, she was full of fun, vivacious, finding every opportunity to go outdoors which she loved, just like yourself, Patrick. This is perhaps what attracted her to you. Such a gusto and love of life but, and I suppose not uncommon in girls her age, she was also selfish with not much regard for others. She was so consumed with her joy of life, as indeed you found out." He looked at Patrick sorrowfully. "I, on the other hand, was quiet and shy, so I was envious of her in many ways, and then she met you and brought you home to meet us. I wanted to be your friend, to be like you instead of the timid, gutless boy that I was then. You, however, only had eyes for Megan, something which I now understand but then I was jealous and even used to follow you both on your trips out. I watched you holding hands as you walked along the banks of the Nile; those early evening walks you used to take."

Patrick smiled as he too remembered them.

"I marvelled at you both and your stamina and energy. I struggled to keep up with you, not being used to the outdoors but I did keep up and very proud of myself I was too. I never really new why I did it; perhaps I wanted to be subconsciously part of your friendship, friends to both of you, something which I had never been able to do and now will never be." His voice was so soft that Patrick was struggling to hear him, but he lifted his head and carried on. "I watched you as you kissed and laughed, enjoying each other's company, but I saw that you were more besotted with Megan than she with you. I knew her behaviour and the little gifts you so lovingly gave her, she would just disregard them, she had no appreciation of their worth or value, not like I would have done. I suppose she couldn't help it, she had always been spoiled as a child, given everything she had wanted, whereas I was left to my own devices, my Mother and Father barely affording me the time of day. I watched as you stood in the moonlight, envious of your closeness which made me feel so lonely and unloved. I used to imagine you and I, Patrick, just talking about things, sharing our interests and not including some girl whose head was full of other things. However, Megan began to change; she had developed her own Avatar world at a very early age, she was the brightest pupil in her group and had been taught through both the computer link at home and a physical study class. When she was with you, Patrick, she still liked the outdoors, but her interest in her computer world was growing stronger and she spent less and less time away from her fantasy world. She developed an obsession with a computer generated character, a Hubot that she had created and if you remember she spent less and less time with you and more time with this Hubot that she had lovingly called Will. I believe that she said goodbye to you because of her love for this Will. She even disregarded her old friend from her early learning days that she had kept in contact with. I can't remember her name but she confided in her a lot. I was furious when I saw her just throw away your almanac, no respect, just disregarded. I saved it. I was angry with her but now I realise she was only young, she didn't mean it, as you were young too, Patrick. I took the almanac and treasured it. I read it from cover to cover and it has only been since meeting Evia that I have been able to recall those memories and feelings. It is so strange to me and yet the power of these emotions is more than I can bear, but I must continue quickly, we don't have much time. Evia said that I would return to my normal self again and my memories would become less clear and harder to recall. You know some of the story: I was taken away and reborn into who I am today, however some of the negative memories did survive, my feelings of jealousy and resentment more heightened than normal. I can only presume that this was due to how I was feeling just before I was taken. I was so consumed by the betrayal by my parents and yes, Megan. I had no remorse or feelings for my actions at the time as I just wanted to make them pay for what they did to me. I retained those memories and they always haunted me sending me into rages so intense that I cannot describe them to you. I ensured that my parents were taken away to the Red Zone for some fabricated excuse. I gave them the same treatment that I was given. They were not given the chance to speak or defend themselves. I ensured that they were left for a short time to wonder their fate and fear for their lives. They were integrated into T.R.I.G.O.M., put into one of the tubes which took body parts, cell by cell and then fed them to where they were needed around the system and to whichever Hubot required them." Patrick could hardly comprehend what he was hearing but remained silent as Braedan continued. "But Megan, she was different, I really wanted her to pay, her death would be too easy. I wanted her to know and suffer, feel alone and frightened just like I did. She was taken on the same day as my parents. She was in her Avatar world so I decided to make sure that she stayed in it permanently but even more cruelly, without her friend Will for company. Her body is in the stasis tube where it is kept alive but she is trapped in her world of Avatar and unable to get out. She is aware of the real world around her and she can see Will but she can never touch him, unable to return to reality. Will's programme was transferred into a living Hubot who I also ensured retained the memories of when they were together so they both share mutual pain and loss."

Patrick shuddered, it had been the body of Megan in that tube and the Hubot which had stood looking in must have been Will. He could not comprehend the suffering she must have and would still be experiencing, endlessly; it was so cruel. At the same time Patrick knew that Braedan was remorseful in his present state and so much of Patrick felt sorry for him, friendless, loveless, both of which he craved so badly; his memories and the part that made him human, cruelly taken away from him until now. These acts of revenge had been taken after his rebirth. Was Michael the human being responsible or Braedan this creation of T.R.I.G.O.M.? Braedan didn't give Patrick a chance to respond, he knew that the Hubots would be activated very soon. "Quickly put on your suit, you must escape."

Patrick quickly grabbed his suit, stumbling in his haste to put it on, his heart pounding as the second Hubot started to move. Braedan, who had been standing talking to Patrick, sat back down at his chair as a sudden pain shot through his head. "Stay still," he shouted to Patrick. The pain in his head was getting worse. "They cannot see you but they will have control over me completely soon so I may not be able to help you. My mission here is to get to the pyramid, destroying anything or anyone who gets in the way. Its secrets and purpose must be found and then destroyed. It is has been classed as a top security threat to T.R.I.G.O.M. When the disc lands you must get out quickly. Do you understand?"

Patrick nodded and just before he covered his head he looked at Braedan. "Thank you, friend."

Braedan could no longer see him and tried to block him from his mind as the tears started to flow. He turned to face the first Hubot and ordered it back to its station before another sharp pain caused him to stumble back with its severity. The disc had landed and quickly Patrick started to move towards the door just as another Hubot's light glowed with the other two. It wouldn't be long before they were all active, he had no time to lose; he had to get out quickly as Braedan had told him. Daylight was flooding into the disc as the door started to slowly open. Patrick made ready to exit but before he did so he turned to check on Braedan. He was now standing tall, surrounded by the Hubots. Patrick knew he was lost again, those piercing blue eyes were shining bright looking straight at him, emotionless and cold. But was he mistaken, there was still something different about him, perhaps he would return again but there was no time to reflect. He jumped the small distance from the door to the ground and ran as fast as he could towards the pyramid. The small ocean that had surrounded the pyramid looked smaller. He noticed a strange mist as some of the water was evaporating. The landscape looked completely different to how he had remembered it. He stopped for a moment to take in these changes but as the ground started to shake vigorously under his feet, his thoughts once again focused on the pyramid and he started to run as fast as he could. He heard Josh's voice as he got nearer. The vibrations from the pyramids were getting stronger, its strength such that Patrick had lost his footing a few times and had nearly fallen to the ground. It was getting harder to run but sheer determination forced him on. Behind he could now hear the humming noise that the Hubots made as they glided over the ground, they were getting closer. He could see the pyramid in the distance. Still surrounded by some water, it kept fading in and out of sight as if it were in some sort of force field. He knew he had to distract the Hubots away from it, he was trying to think what to do and then suddenly Admar was in front of him.

Chapter Forty-Five

Joshua and Torri were stood looking despondent staring at each other with all the burden of the world on their shoulders. Disbelief that they had come so far and had now failure. Words would not come. Torri looked at Josh with despair, her eyes starting to fill with her tears. It was then that Evia appeared before them, outlined in light with no physical form, the pull and swirl of the remaining water not affecting her at all. They both jumped back as if they had been struck by lightning.

"You must hurry for you do not have long." She spoke without words but the words formed in their mind so that they knew what she had said. Josh looked at her, unable to speak, just holding on to Torri as if he was afraid to let her go. Evia continued. "Do not be afraid, I am here to protect you until you are both safe. I cannot be harmed but you two are still in danger and so we must hurry with the last symbol which will ensure your safety."

Torri looked again at the bracelet hoping that perhaps by magic another symbol had appeared. Evia smiled, she knew their anguish. "You have the last symbol." She turned to look at Josh. Patrick's old good luck charm had started to glow around his neck. Patrick had kept it safe all these years not realising its importance. They both looked in realisation, this was the final symbol. Neither of them questioned Evia, not understanding but knowing that they must hurry and that it was important. Torri reached towards Josh, her fingers starting to tremble; this was the last symbol. She hesitated for a split second but then as she touched it, her whole body began to tingle and a loud rushing noise which was followed by that haunting music as before filled the air. The last symbol took its rightful place with the others. Instantly the whole of the pyramid began to vibrate and its shell of old decaying stone began to change. The old crumbling stone was no more, instead it had completely metamorphosed. It was smooth, not made of stone but shone so brightly and they both realised it was made completely of gold, as if it had come directly from the stars. The top of the pyramid seemed to be encrusted with what looked like precious stones. They recognised some as Emeralds, Diamonds, Opals and Sapphires; all adorning its peak. Others they did not readily recognise, but such was their beauty. The small ocean which had surrounded the pyramid a few moments ago was no more, it had now completely vanished as if it had never existed and they were standing, instead, on a long, wide path made completely of marble. It was not cold to the touch but emanated warmth which they could feel under their feet. This grand path was inset with more precious stones, all along the edges of it, forming perfect straight lines leading to the pyramid. They looked closer at the golden structure and could vaguely make out markings which were set into the gold. The vibrations were getting stronger and as they did so, the markings became clearer. Set within the gold were carvings which resembled branches of a tree, they looked so intricate and whether it was a trick of the light, they appeared to be moving as if they had life of their own. The shapes of the branches were straight, with many smaller offsets, all leading up towards the top of the pyramid. Its beauty was breathtaking and all the twists and turns of each intricate branch seemed to have purpose and meaning. The pyramid began to slowly turn, appearing to be on a central pivot and moved effortlessly. They both remained still as it moved, watching with wonder as it turned. It looked as if it was the most natural thing for it to do. The second side of the pyramid was now facing them. They could see that this side also looked like a golden living tree but its branches were formed differently than the first side. They were not so straight and lacked some of the beauty. It turned again to reveal the third side of the pyramid which at first glance, appeared to have no such markings. Its surface was seemingly flat and smooth, however, as they looked closer they could just make out faint lines, not so clearly defined as the other two sides and without life. It turned again, returning to its original position. Suddenly the slab holding the symbols started to slide to one side, revealing a large aperture. They stood still just looking into the darkness of the opening, still held spellbound with the awesome sight of this magnificent structure. The smaller pyramids close by had also started to vibrate but before they could look to see what was happening, they saw the Air Disc hovering some distance away. It started to descend at great velocity, landing with precision, its door slowly opening. They couldn't at first make out what was happening; it kept disappearing in and out of vision in sequence with the pyramid which was also beginning to fade as the vibrations and magnetic force which had bound it to the Earth was beginning to change. The illusion that it was an ancient crumbling pyramid had disguised it for thousands of years in readiness for this day when it would be needed once again. It had created interest and speculation for the world's peoples and had inspired imagination and theories for its purpose but none had ever come close to its true origin and relevance to life.

Chapter Forty-Six

Patrick stopped running and Admar spoke hurriedly. "They still can't see you but we must keep them away from the pyramid so we must show ourselves to them to buy some time."

Patrick nodded. He knew what he had to do and started to take off his suit. He looked at Admar in wonder as he started to transform from light to his physical body but he didn't have much time to take in this wonder as the Hubots, who could now detect him, were closing in fast. Patrick looked over again at the pyramid as it kept changing from its usual form to a shiny new structure that he did not recognise. It was almost like it was pulsating as it changed from one form to another, fading in and out of view, it looked like it was disappearing. "Run now, Patrick," Admar shouted, distracting him from looking at the Great Pyramid. "Head towards the smaller pyramids, you will be safe." Patrick did not argue, he trusted Admar explicitly and so without hesitation he changed direction. The Hubots followed hot in pursuit. Patrick ran so fast that he felt that his heart was going to beat out of his chest. He could sense that they were still behind him and it was only as he had nearly reached the first small pyramid, he realised that Admar was no longer with him. He reached the pyramid, stopping to get his breath, not knowing what to do next. He looked over towards the large pyramid and there he saw his friend, Joshua with Torri. Admar with Evia was standing with them. They all looked so still, almost like statues and then he could see Josh and Torri no more.

Josh and Torri felt themselves seemingly floating towards the opening and into the dark passage. They could not move or resist, their bodies were compelled to enter but they felt no panic or fear as they entered through the aperture together. As soon as they reached the inside, it was as light as a bright sunny day and they felt warmth on their skin as if their bodies were being caressed by sunlight. The energy which had been compelling them to enter the pyramid through the aperture had now subsided and they were both in full control of their movements. The passageway was made of Jasper. It was bright and welcoming giving off its own light with the most amazing speckles of red and green, unlike anything they had ever seen before and the straight line of precious stones had continued through from the outside. The vibrations were getting stronger and Josh glanced back to the outside world. It had gone dark but he could see no stars or light in the sky. He shuddered even though he was not cold. They continued their journey, deeper inside the pyramid, the walls changing as they walked further. Every type of mineral and stone in existence seemed to be incorporated into the walls of this passageway. Josh recognised some of them through his work and his studies of the Earth, which assisted him in his passion for ancient objects and their origins. Within no time they reached the end of the passage and it opened out. What they saw took their breath away. As they looked to the right there was the most wonderful sight. Was this perhaps the real garden of Eden, or the gardens of Babylon foretold in the Bible? The tree of life, everything that was life and beauty was to behold in this place, which seemed not to have any boundaries. Its space appeared to be endless. It had an atmosphere of its own, the temperature not too hot or cold. As they looked to the left they saw another building. "The hall of records," Evia whispered. "Every genetic code of life kept safe as it was when everything was created," she continued. "This has been the giver of life to this planet, created its atmosphere and created its gravity. The pyramid remains in its constant position within space, it is everything else that will change around it. Each life changing Epoch that has existed on Earth has marked its exterior, their indentions show on the outside of the pyramid or as we know it, the Star of Life. Each life cycle is shown as you would see a tree with its branches showing their progression or regression as the case may be. Now however it is time for the next major change and our Star must turn again. Admar and I have done our time and will go home for our final rest."

"But who are you?" Torri was the first to speak.

"We have been known throughout history and time as many names. You will know us only from this last Epoch, from the ancient writings as Adam and Eve. Now new history will be recorded again, giving life chance to start again and advance. Nothing dies, only changes, but it will be you that will be written in the great books of truth when the new era comes to pass. For it is you who will remain safe, nurturing new life which will be adapted for a different environment, waiting for everything to be made ready. Come, sit and all will be revealed …

Chapter Forty-Seven

Patrick had started to panic. The Hubots were nearly upon him, when Admar suddenly appeared again. This time Patrick was not alarmed. He was getting used to these strange events and Admar's sudden disappearances and reappearances. "Quick, Patrick, take my hand. Josh and Torri are safe now, they cannot be harmed. We must now concentrate on those that are left."

"Those that are left?" Patrick questioned. As Patrick had taken Admar's hand he had felt a vibration flow through his body and although the Hubots were still there it was as if the world was slightly out of synchronisation and time had momentarily stopped. Even the severe weather was unable to penetrate them and the Hubots were moving in slow motion.

Admar continued. "Things are about to change but there is time. We are only just beginning to pave the way. You are still able to help those who you would wish to."

"Megan," Patrick almost shouted. It was an instantaneous response and he had not even thought about Josh and Torri. Admar had said they were safe and that was enough for him, such was his complete trust in him.

"If you want to save Megan, then we must return to T.R.I.G.O.M. You can use the air disc. All of the Hubots are out in their vain attempt to destroy the pyramid and capture your friends. Our work here is done for the moment. Come, I will lead you to the air disc. They cannot see you at present, keep hold of my hand." In no time they had reached the air disc; the door had been left open in their haste to pursue Patrick. Admar let go of Patrick and immediately the vibration he had felt tingling through his body stopped and everything which had been in slow motion, reverted back to its usual pace. He looked over towards the Hubots as they seemed to be in some confusion as to where Patrick had vanished to. He quickly boarded the air disc; Admar was already inside. He had his hands over the computer terminal and amazingly had full control of the disc as it started to generate its energy ready for take-off. Patrick quickly looked out towards the large pyramid, suddenly feeling the urge to check if Josh and Torri were safe. As he looked over at the pyramid he could only just make out its form. It was fading in and out of view again. As it faded he could see the landscape which had been behind it so clearly as if nothing was there and then it appeared again blocking out the view. Each time it faded away, the storm grew stronger and the lightning grew more intense. Just then a lightning bolt hit the ground and the unfortunate Hubot in its wake didn't stand a chance. Patrick looked at Admar with concern. "It's OK," he reassured him. "We have time to go back. Josh and Torri are safe and the pyramid will not be gone from sight completely yet, not until the time is right."

The air disc shot upwards with great velocity and Patrick briefly saw the Hubots turning quickly around towards the disc; the smoking remains of their comrade strewn over the ground. Within seconds they were out of view heading back to the Red Zone. He could just imagine their confusion and disbelief at their lack of control. He allowed himself a smile even though the panic he felt inside was getting harder and harder to squash. They were travelling at an unprecedented speed. It only seemed like a few minutes and they were beginning to dock at the landing site. Patrick had expected to be greeted by raging Hubots, but it was quiet and looked deserted. Patrick looked at Admar questioningly. Admar smiled at him. "We have travelled at light speed and so have been able to arrive here a little in the future. The Hubots are not here, they have left for safety but they have left everything else here, including Megan." He touched Patrick's arm reassuringly. "Do not worry, we are not too late. Come." With that the door of the Air Disc opened and they quickly got out. Admar seemed to know exactly where to go but beckoned Patrick to hurry as another crack of lightning lit up the skies above them. The sky was a strange reddish colour and Patrick had lost track now and didn't know if it was night or day. He quickly followed Admar. They had entered the big red doors, which had opened instantly at Admar's command. Patrick shivered as he passed tube after tube; the painful memories of his experience darkening his thoughts. Admar stopped suddenly. Directly in front of them a Hubot was standing staring at one of the tubes. It looked lifeless, no light was emanating from it and it was standing so still. Admar and Patrick had stopped in their tracks. Patrick hardly dared breathe but Admar pointed to the tube and they slowly moved towards it. The Hubot stirred but made no attempt to stop them as they reached the tube. Patrick put his hands towards the tube and as his hand got nearer the colouring inside began to change from a dark thick blue liquid to a more transparent substance and as his hand reached the surface of the tube it became almost as clear as water. It was then that Patrick saw her, or something that resembled her. "Megan," he whispered, the Hubot turned round and looked directly at Patrick. A faint light glowed from its form but nothing that appeared menacing. Just then the whole building shook as yet another earthquake devoured the Earth's crust increasing its fragility. The tube started to shake with the force of the shock waves that ensued and Patrick had to grab on to Admar's arm to steady himself. As the liquid inside the tube became less turbulent, the form inside became clearer and now it was Admar that reached out to touch the tube. As he touched the tube, the liquid became still as a bright white light flowed from his hands and surrounded the tube. Patrick stared incredulously as the liquid within it evaporated, leaving a small fragile looking being at the bottom of the tube. The light flowed stronger now, becoming more intense and giving off a sound not unlike the crackling of a lightning strike. The light had now completely engulfed the lifeless body in the tube and for a short time, Patrick could not make out the body as the light formed an oval shield around it. Suddenly the light vanished and Admar let go of the tube. As he let go the surface of the tube disappeared and Patrick could not believe what he saw. The body in the tube had vanished and the Hubot was no longer. In its place there she stood.

"Megan," Patrick whispered. She looked at Patrick, her eyes full of tears as she held out her hands to him. Patrick hesitated for a moment, still in shock, but then took her hands and hugged her so tight as his eyes filled with tears. It seemed like all the emotion of the last few days had come to the surface and he found himself sobbing uncontrollably as he held tightly on to Megan.

Admar had stood back and allowed Patrick this time and then he gently put his hand on his shoulder. "Come now, Patrick, it is time to go," he said softly but with an urgency that Patrick understood. He handed a robe to Patrick to give to Megan, which Patrick promptly wrapped around her. Megan, who had been clinging to Patrick desperately, was now feeling the warmth of the garment that was wrapped around her. She was shivering and looked very weak and when she tried to speak no words would come out. Admar now spoke to her. "You will be alright now. I know that you have been imprisoned, your mind in fantasy and your body here in this tube for many years. I know your despair but you are set free now but we must hurry and get out of here. We have to find Braedan." As he spoke his name, Megan began to shake, a look of fear and horror on her face. "You will be safe." Admar spoke again and touched her face. This seemed to calm her and she just nodded with acceptance. Patrick didn't understand why they needed to find Braedan but he was beyond asking questions. He felt tired and just wanted to wake up from this nightmare. Would anything ever be normal again? Would those carefree days ever return? He thought not and knowing this he felt such an overwhelming sadness that he had to shake himself so that he could carry on. "Come." Admar pointed towards the doors. Patrick, without thinking, scooped Megan up in his arms, wrapping his arms around her and quickly heading in the direction of the Air Disc.

Chapter Forty-Eight

Megan was as light as a feather and had not put up any protest at being carried. Patrick had just known intuitively that this was the right thing to do. They quickened their pace as the ground rumbled below them. Admar's face was stern, indicating the urgency to get safely back to the Air Disc. The doors once again opened as they approached and as he looked down at Megan again, he remembered the love that he had felt for her all those years ago. Those memories were never lost, they had just been buried with time; there always in moments of reflection on the rare occasions he had time to himself, or the melancholy moods he sometimes drifted into when things were not going so well. He had never really felt the same about anyone else. He had had a few relationships, the longest had been a girl called Ellie and a smile touched his lips as he remembered. He had panicked when she had wanted more from him as he was just not ready and had quickly distanced himself from her until she had finally given up on him. She was a sweet girl, but much too consumed with the modern world and had no interest in the outdoors and in particular, Patrick's love of the past. Their relationship really didn't stand a chance. After Ellie, he stuck to his usual style of a few dates and a good time, after that he would become bored and move on. Strange he was thinking of the past now, amidst this time of utter chaos. It made him want to laugh through sheer panic and fear.

Megan was looking up at Patrick. She felt so cold, so strange feeling the sensation of controlling her body again. She felt so heavy and it was an effort to move her eyes. She wanted to speak but had no energy to speak. Patrick, Patrick. She wanted to shout to him but no words would come. She wanted to thank him for rescuing her, to say sorry that she had hurt him. She had been a young girl when she had met Patrick but had felt an instant connection to him. Their friendship had been easy, their conversation flowed naturally and their adolescent love grew quickly. Perhaps had they been left alone things would have turned out differently but Braedan had not allowed that. Her eyes filled with tears as she thought of Braedan. She had loved her brother once but now could feel nothing, not even hatred for what he had done to her and how he had made her suffer all these years. She couldn't help but think that he had suffered more because of it. Somewhere deep down in his being, there must be remorse for what he had done. Jealousy; that pitiful, all consuming emotion had been their downfall and had lost them everything, the cost of which was immeasurable. Then she felt the gentle touch of Patrick's hand on her cheek and the tears from her eyes touched his fingers. He drew her close wrapping her in his arms, she felt safe and allowed herself to sleep.

"Quickly." Admar was urging Patrick to hurry again as they quickly entered the Air Disc. They had no time to strap themselves in as the ground below started to give way, Admar hastily took control and they shot upwards away from the dangers of the ground. Trying not to stumble as their hasty ascent made the Air Disc less stable, he gently laid Megan down safely on one of the long seats which then automatically moulded to her body to keep her secure. He looked down at her again, not wanting to take his eyes off her. He needed to know that she was alright; he badly wanted to protect her. He eventually managed to pull himself away to sit securely next to Admar as this ride was going to be rocky. Patrick looked out of the many windows in the disc. The lightning lit the sky like a furnace. He was sure he had never seen anything like it. Not even the Polar Aurorae in the Northern Hemisphere could hold so much strange beauty as this. It lit the skies so brightly but with all different colours as the Solar Winds interacted with the atmosphere, the sun storm raging from so far out in space having such a profound effect on the earth. Patrick reflected how the ancient tribes had described those Northern Lights as the "Dance of the Spirits". Patrick could understand why they had thought this but now it was like the spirit of the earth shouting for help. He looked upwards towards the sun; it seemed to be glowing brighter but as his eyes grew accustomed to the brightness, he could make out another light in the sky. It wasn't the sun and it wasn't the moon; it was much larger than the moon. He looked at Admar and pointed to the object, Admar nodded without looking up and Patrick thought he saw a tear fall down Admar's cheek but he was unable to check as just then the Air Disc jerked violently as some debris had hit them and Admar had to manoeuvre quickly to avoid full impact with the object. "What's happening?" Patrick shouted out looking at Admar in panic. Admar didn't answer, he had his eyes closed, seemingly steering the disc to safety with just the power of his mind, blocking out any visual distractions, allowing his mind to be focused. Patrick tried to calm himself and shut his eyes, he would try to think of something or somewhere else. He took deep breaths; he needed to keep calm … He was back in his youth at the time when he had first met Megan, she was holding his hand chattering away about her day. He had loved to hear her voice and share in the enthusiasm of everything that she had done that day. He didn't even try to get a word in, it made him smile. She had just seen a friend that she had first met at her learning centre and she was eagerly telling Patrick all about her. "She is very special, she knows things which haven't happened yet and she is so interesting." Patrick had only half been listening, as he was taking in the moment of her hair gently blowing in the wind as she talked. He did wonder what she had meant by that but he just put it down to girlish fantasies. He remembered now that she had spoken about this girl quite often. Why had he not taken any notice of this at the time? He breathed in deeper trying to remember … yes, she had described her as special and she had often told Megan that she had spoken to people who were not here in the physical world, as she described it and that one day she would be called upon for some great purpose. He remembered laughing to himself as Megan had gone on to tell him that she could also speak to her dead grandfather and often saw the image of a boy she knew she would meet one day but he lived far away and his name would begin with a J... Patrick's eyes opened. Could Megan's special friend be Torri? And then he remembered Braedan had mentioned her special friend too. The Air Disc now was vibrating badly as lightning struck. Admar's control was getting weaker, he could barely keep it from plummeting downwards. "I have to land it here." His thought was in Patrick's head. He understood but got up from his seat and kneeling down to cover Megan with his body to protect her, as he waited for the impact of the ground to hit.

Chapter Forty-Nine

The Air Disc landed without its usual softness but Admar's skill had lessened the impact, Patrick still shielding Megan as the craft shook from its contact with the Earth. They had not been able to keep up the speed which they had travelled at on their journey to the Red Zone and Patrick had lost all his bearings regarding time. He looked at Megan, checking that she was OK. She smiled back at him to let him know she was alright, he gently stroked her cheek before standing up and as he did so he looked over at Admar. Admar looked at him to reassure him although he too looked a little shaken after the experience but managed to whisper softly to Patrick, "It's OK, I just need a little time to recover. I have been in this atmosphere for too long and so I just need to regain my strength."

Patrick looked at him with concern, he remembered well his first meeting with Admar and his own feelings of dizziness and disorientation when he had visited his office, that place in the caves, existing in a different vibration, a world within a world. Patrick looked at Admar and noticed with relief he was starting to regain his colour. He certainly looked much better now. Megan lay fast asleep overtaken by her exhaustion. In this moment, when time seemed to be standing still, a serene stillness surrounded them blocking out the chaos of the world. Patrick felt calm as he looked at Admar. "Please tell me more of what is happening. Do we have a future? Will we survive this"?

Knowing that they were safe in what appeared to be like a time bubble Admar turned to Patrick and nodded. "Yes I will explain a little more to you but I am very tired and speech is very tiring for me so please sit back and close your eyes. I will transfer my words to your thoughts it will be easier."

Patrick accepted this without question, he had experienced too many strange things to even be remotely surprised at this request and so he relaxed back, as best he could and closed his eyes.

As Admar's words came into his mind, he could see in vivid colour everything he described; his words became alive. Patrick could feel, hear and sense everything as if he were there. Admar began.

Planet Earth has been destined to host 7 Epochs of life and our current time is nearing the end. This is the sixth, we have one more to go. After each Epoch, only limited information was passed down from the previous time to ensure progression of the spirit. The limitations were needed to allow new thoughts and stimulate growth which would not be too heavily influenced by the past but just enough to ensure that physical life could continue. Each age has been inspired by ancient knowledge. For instance fables and relics were some of the ways that information was passed down, left open to interpretation or to be dismissed by free minds.

Patrick's thoughts went straight to the biblical telling of the first human beings Adam and Eve. In his mind he was there, he could smell the most exquisite aroma, surrounded by fragrant flowers, the likes of which he had never seen before. He was there in the Garden of Eden. As he looked around he realised it wasn't just a garden, it was a world; it was a planet, not unlike Earth in its size but the magnitude of its colours and its beauty were beyond words. Earth held no comparison to its wonders, a poorer version of this wonderful place. Yes, Admar's words formed in his head; this is where the story of the Garden of Eden comes from.

It is not a myth but an actual place foretold in a story so that it would never be forgotten, a place that was recreated on Earth. The stories get distorted with time but the important parts of a story always remain and this works well to preserve important knowledge. Evia and I or Adam and Eve as the story goes, were not banished from this place but were chosen to nurture life here on Earth by taking some of our knowledge with us. However we cannot speak in our own language on Earth, as we are from a different time, in another universe requiring a different time flow, so our words could never be used or understood and so the first method of communication was made through symbols before language evolved. These sacred symbols were contained in Torri's bracelet, the keys to the pyramid and the only way to reveal its true form and purpose, but only by those with the correct genetic code. Only those of the old order, which includes Torri and Joshua, have this code. The pyramid aids us to travel back and forth between our two worlds, it controls the connection between the two and many others, power beyond even my comprehension. We have had help from others, who have visited the Earth in times of need. You have recorded them in your history in many ways, sometimes referring to them as Gods or Angels, in many books; the Bible, the Koran, the book of Enoch to name but a few. These stories inspired many but have also been the basis for destruction because it is always a choice and the human spirit is free to decide its future. Some worldly events have been described as good and evil whilst others a clash between Negative and Positive, or action and consequence, cause and effect but I can tell you there are rules too of this universe. There are many universes which are intertwined with each other. So many that you would not comprehend how they work, however it is only important for you to know that the seventh Epoch will soon be upon us and a different future for us all. Braedan will come into his own with your help, Patrick. This is your destiny with the help of Megan who has gone through so much but because of this she will understand and be of great importance and value to you.

Patrick saw Megan in his mind, a beautiful young woman with no trace of the horror and nightmare that she had undergone.

Admar continued ... but already the way has to be prepared for a time that will come and this last Epoch is different for the Earth's time will be done and then the next planet will host life. Evia and I prepared the way so many millions of years ago, so too will Joshua and Torri.

Chapter Fifty

Admar's words were still appearing in Patrick's mind has he continued with his explanation. Both Evia and I, still dwell in our vibration, we can walk amongst you without harm, surviving your atmosphere for a limited time before we have to return. We are always here but sometimes in another space time, a higher vibration as you would understand it, only our light is visible to you. If you look up into the night sky you will often see a glow surrounding the moon, a halo of light. That is our light which still connects us to you. You will always be able to see it and it will give you comfort in the years to come.

Patrick opened his eyes, Admar was smiling at him. "But what about Josh and Torri?" He was once again concerned about his friends, panic starting to get the better of him, completely destroying the calmness he had just felt. He knew instantly to close his eyes, the calmness returning to him as his mind once again submitted to Admar.

Joshua and Torri are young as you know them now, but they have been here on the Earth many times for they are the chosen ones, they themselves chose to take life forward, to nurture and prepare for the next planet, which will take the place of the Earth when its time is done. You must understand that nothing dies, just changes and so it must be. Torri and Joshua will remember who they were in previous lives as will you, Patrick. Once they return to the pyramid all of their memories and all of the knowledge that they have acquired will be with them again. All destinies are eventually fulfilled and it is just the choice of roads to take that may vary along the way. Some choices making the way easier and some harder, whatever the case may be but there is always a reason and always a consequence. There have been many civilisations here on Earth, some you have no records of. Some had more knowledge than you have now, computers all the things that you think are only of this modern age and yet you have only reached a relatively low level of intelligence. You too, Patrick, will remember one day, that it was your choice to do what you are about to do and all will be well. The pyramids, which is your name for them and there are many in the universes, are anchorage points controlling time flows and stability, providing the planet with its Life. Like trees provide you with oxygen, so the pyramid provides you with life; your own tree of life. It gives your Earth gravity to sustain your life form, your protective layer from space and much more than you can imagine. However, all actions, negative, positive, good, evil are absorbed by it. The markings on its side denote the progression that each Epoch has made or not made. All actions have consequence like I said but I can tell you no more on that, there are things even beyond my knowledge.

Patrick opened his eyes again as Megan started to stir. He instinctively stroked her cheek, which seemed to comfort her and her sleep continued. He knew enough now to realise that they must return and although the world to him would never be the same again, it would be a beginning of a new age and he could take comfort in the fact that he knew it was not the end. Admar now spoke with words. "Come, we need to carry on. I have ensured that the air disc is repaired and that we will return to the appropriate moment in time and place."

They sat back in their seats as Admar took control of the Air Disc. Megan had woken now and Patrick had made sure she was safely moulded into the flight seat ready for take-off. He had tenderly planted a kiss on her forehead before making his way to his own seat. She smiled at him and his heart melted. The Air Disc rose up with its usual swiftness and started its journey. It gathered up speed as it hovered above the Earth but then suddenly it gathered up speed gaining with such velocity the like of which Patrick had never experienced before. He could see only strange shapes and lights around him, the Earth invisible to his sight as he clung to his chair for reassurance. He trusted Admar implicitly but even so his heart had started to pound in his chest and his knuckles were beginning to turn white as he gripped his chair harder. He turned to look at Megan. She had her eyes closed and he wasn't sure if she was sleeping again or was trying not to show her fear. Gradually the Air Disc started to slow down and the lights started to fade and the Earth emerged below them, Patrick let out a sigh of relief which made Admar smile. The Air Disc had now stopped and was hovering over the familiar shape of the pyramid. Patrick looked closer and realised that the pyramid was its usual crumbling self, not the beautiful golden wonder that it had revealed when Torri and Joshua had entered it.

Chapter Fifty-One

Patrick looked down on the familiar landscape as they still hovered above the ground, the waters of the small ocean gently lapping the sides of the pyramid caused by the slight air disturbance that the Air Disc was creating. Admar knew the question that Patrick was about to ask. "When Joshua and Torri opened the pyramid, its true glory was revealed, closing again when they were safely inside. The Gateway can only remain open for a short time until once again it is veiled from this world. You can only see the illusion of an old relic, giving the impression it was built by some ancient civilisation, but it is still there in its glory. It is alive within its own time and space ensuring that Earth is still docked in its safe grip allowing this planet to maintain its life source which it will do so until the earth's time is done. Without it you could not survive or have even existed. So many have tried to solve the riddle of how the pyramids were built, or for what purpose, no one has ever got close to the truth. The success of human evolution is recorded on its very substance and from which maybe all our fate is ultimately judged but I do not know the answer to that. You now look down at the familiar landscape and you will never see the pyramid in its true form again. Your job is here and now. Braedan and Megan need you, for you are as important as Joshua and Torri. They have their own destiny which will last many years into the future but yours is here and now. The Earth's slow change will become accelerated and the poles will shift once again. This will not mean total death and destruction but it will be a time for adaption. Braedan who still has his human brain functions but also possesses a reinforced body which is made of many elements will be of valuable help to you to ensure your safety until you have achieved what is required of you. We can thank T.R.I.G.O.M. for that." Admar smiled. "Braedan will be the key and you must help him now to find himself again and to do the great things that he is capable of. He needs your guidance. He needs the love of Megan and yourself and within the process of this you too will find great rewards. I must leave you very soon but I will bring Evia with me to see you; our time here is nearly done." He let out a long, tired sigh.

Patrick looked at Admar, this kind special man of whom he had grown very fond. He had given him strength and courage when he had needed it most, he had helped him find a strength that he had not known he had possessed. He could sense the great service this man had given to mankind and he could only wonder at the sacrifices he must have made. He exuded a great sadness about him as he looked back at Patrick before quickly looking away and closing his eyes to concentrate. The Air Disc started to descend, finally landing at the lake's edge, not too far from where Joshua and Torri had, not so long ago, entered the water for their final swim to the pyramid. The landing was very smooth but Megan began to stir as the Air Disc touched down. Patrick instinctively went over to her to make sure that she was OK, giving her reassurance. She smiled up him, his face full of concern. Once he was sure that she was alright, Patrick looked back to Admar as the doors of the Air Disc started to open.

"What about the Hubots? I know that Braedan was lost to T.R.I.G.O.M. again!"

Again Admar transferred his thoughts straight to Patrick. "Don't worry, we are a little ahead of the time from which we left and Braedan is once again himself and able to control T.R.I.G.O.M. but your technology, computers, whatever you name them, will not survive the changes that will come. You will see for yourself. Now I leave you but I will see you soon." He sounded a little impatient. Perhaps he was getting tired again, Patrick thought and so he quickly held out his hand to Megan. Admar smiled over at him, of course, Patrick knew instantly that he could read his thoughts and his smile acknowledged the fact that he was grateful for his understanding. Megan slowly stood up, still a little weak as she gripped his hand. She needed his support but the rate in which she was regaining her strength was remarkable, considering her ordeal. Patrick jumped down from the disk and lifted Megan safely to the ground. They moved away from the Air Disc as the doors closed and it started to slowly rise up. Then suddenly, it vanished. Patrick wasn't sure if it had risen quickly or just simply disappeared, perhaps into Admar's own world and time. He was not surprised at anything these days but after it disappeared he was left with a feeling of calmness which seemed to surround him. He felt that again he was being helped even without consciously seeing or hearing anyone. This gave him comfort as he started to look around him.

Chapter Fifty-Two

Patrick looked over at the large pyramid which made the smaller ones near to it fade into insignificance.

He remembered what Admar had told him about earlier times and some of the ancient civilisations that had inhabited and flourished on this planet. They had marvelled and speculated over this great structure, some had even worshiped it giving way to sacrifice and magical practices. As it had been the only structure in the very beginning, it had been revered by the ancient people who believed it to have magical powers and be in some way connected to the stars. Perhaps they had been closer than they had thought to its true origin. As intelligence and skills developed over time, the ancient peoples, such as the Egyptians and the Mayans, had tried to replicate its mysteries. Although these smaller structures held no comparison to the true form and purpose of the pyramid, they were certainly a tribute to their skills, mathematical and architectural prowess. Nothing of that nature would be even attempted in this modern age even if there was any interest to do so, which there was definitely not. Modern age, Patrick sighed to himself, feeling such sadness as he realised that the human race had regressed far more than they could possibly imagine and that worse than ever was that no one even cared. What should be important had been forgotten, the purpose of being alive had become worthless with a dependence on an artificial intelligence that had been created by people who still had that thirst for learning and knowledge. At what point did they give up and let machines take over? He could only speculate perhaps it was the way that it was supposed to be, after all, and again Admar's words came to him. T.R.I.G.O.M. had created Braedan who would be of importance. Was everything planned? His mind was beginning to work overtime and his thoughts were not so clear. He shook himself and looked over at Megan, there was work to do and he remembered clearly Admar saying that they must find Braedan. As he had stood contemplating how he was going to find him, he realised he was finding it harder and harder to breathe. Megan too was struggling and at one point he thought that they were both going to faint. The air was so thick and he was finding it hard to hear or get his bearings. A hand suddenly touched his shoulder making him jump, his heart pounding as he spun around to face whoever or whatever it was.

Chapter Fifty-Three

Braedan stood before him. There were no signs of the Hubots, as Patrick came face to face with him, those blue eyes staring into his. He flinched back and Megan screamed out loud, regaining her voice, making them both jump.

"It's OK," Braedan said, his eyes softening as he looked at them both. "I am in control of myself now and have still retained my memories of the past and my childhood all thanks to Evia. T.R.I.G.O.M. played its part in creating me which means I have a vast knowledge and extra human functions at my disposal. I am probably the first of a new being and so I am learning to celebrate it rather than despise, hate and all the other negative thoughts that I had been consumed with." Patrick breathed a sigh of relief but before he had time to ask anything Braedan spoke quickly. "A lot has happened since you left. I know you must be confused as when you last saw me I was surrounded by Hubots but you have been gone longer than you think, it is exactly one month since you vanished."

Patrick nearly choked with the shock, he had known that they had travelled at what must have been light speed and Admar had not been too sure of the exact time they had arrived back but he was thinking probably hours, certainly not a month. At this point Megan, who had been afraid and standing behind Patrick, moved to his side; she was feeling stronger and stronger all the time. Braedan looked at her apprehensively, he knew the wrong that he had done her and was expecting her retribution. Instead, she held her arms out to him and he fell like a helpless child into her arms. Until that moment he had not been able to cry, he was unsure if those emotions were still within him. They now surfaced and he found comfort in their release. Patrick stood back and gave them the space and time that they needed. No words were uttered as they were unnecessary, they just held each other and felt the forgiveness, the sorrow and the happiness that emanated from their beings flow through them. After some time, Megan stood back and Braedan had to take a minute to compose himself as these powerful emotions flooding through his being had taken him a little off balance. After what Patrick thought to be a respectable amount of time, he gently asked Braedan what had happened after they had gone. He noticed that the weather conditions had become more severe. When they first alighted from the Air Disc the air felt heavy and humid but in a short space of time they had been standing, the light had faded, giving way to a strange red glow and he could hear what he thought to be the faint sound of thunder in the far distance. The lake, surrounding the pyramid was starting to ripple as the breeze intensified causing small waves, which broke as they touched the pyramid's sides.

Braedan had composed himself and Megan was once again standing beside Patrick, slipping her hand into his to which he responded with a gentle squeeze. Braedan pointed over to a small vehicle, which they had not noticed before. "I think we should go somewhere a little safer. The climate is changing and you will be finding it harder to breathe." Patrick nodded.

Braedan continued. "There is a strong electrical storm on its way and I think we should get back to base. I will fill you in there."

"Back to base?" Patrick asked. He had no plans to return to T.R.I.G.O.M. headquarters, he had seen far too much of that place and shuddered with the memories of the Red Zone. He could also feel Megan's anguish at the thought of returning and instinctively put his arm around her. This reaction was not lost on Braedan and he actually understood their fear and was quick to reassure them.

"Don't worry, T.R.I.G.O.M. is no threat to you now as I will explain later and I understand your reluctance to go back there. I have just thought of another place that we can go. It's a place where I used to go to try and find the peace which had for so long eluded me. Come and you will see. I know that it's difficult and considering my past conduct I realise that it will be hard but can you both find it in your hearts to trust me? I mean you no harm as I only want a chance to make up for the many wrongs that have been done to you and in fact what has been done to us all."

Patrick and Megan looked at each other and nodded at Braedan. His relief at their decision showing on his face as he actually smiled at them. He looked so much happier, his smile lit up his face to show a side to him that Patrick had never seen before. His smile quickly disappeared as a flash of lightning lit up the sky. "Quick, we must hurry, it's not far from here but we need to get going before the storm breaks."

They started to walk, following Braedan as he pointed towards a distant object. "That's our vehicle, hurry." The breeze was getting stronger by the second. They could not make out what the vehicle was as they needed to keep their heads down as they battled against the elements. Megan was walking as fast as she could and although she was getting stronger all the time, she was still considerably weaker than Patrick and Braedan. The breeze had turned into a strong wind now as they heard the waves angrily hitting the sides of the pyramid. The force of the wind was making the short distance to the vehicle harder, blowing directly at them in gale force gusts. Braedan stayed in front of them, his body shielding them from its force as much as it could. They were all getting tired, it was so hard to breathe. Then Braedan shouted loudly, so that they could hear above the noise of the wind. "We are here. You can stop."

Patrick froze, a look of astonishment on his face. He couldn't believe his eyes, it was his old car. "Quick, get in," Braedan ordered, opening the car doors. As quickly as they could they threw themselves in, slamming the car doors shut. Patrick and Megan could hardly breathe. Braedan of course, did not feel the effects of the elements and Patrick realised Braedan would be able to survive these harsh conditions much longer than they could. Braedan deftly manoeuvred himself into the driver's seat and started the engine but he looked a little worried as he turned around to make sure that they were safely seated and secured. "This may be a little bumpy. I hadn't realised the severity of this storm and the electrical disturbance is highly charged, so please hold tight."

Patrick was confused. Why his car and not one of the air discs that Braedan must have the use of?

Braedan leant over to him as Patrick was sat in the front passenger seat. "I will explain later."

The car set off on the rugged path, where it had been parked, swaying from the strong wind that was creating such turbulent conditions. The storm was getting stronger. They were secure in their seats but the car was struggling to battle the elements. Braedan was looking concerned as he shouted over to Patrick, "I am not sure whether we will make it all the way in this."

Patrick suddenly remembered the Cave of Symbols near the coffee booth. Surely a cave would be the best place to take refuge from this severe storm and it wouldn't take too long to get to. He was sure that there was a road leading partially to the cave; the rest of the way they would have to walk. He told Braedan about the cave. He nodded his head and smiled. That was the direction in which they were heading, the place that Braedan was taking them if the old car could manage the task in hand.

Chapter Fifty-Four

Braedan knew exactly where the Cave of Symbols was. He had never been inside since he had become part of T.R.I.G.O.M. The caves always had a strange effect on him. Since his meeting with Evia and his memories had been restored, he remembered he had visited them as boy. He remembered looking at the strange symbols on its walls, marvelling at their simplistic design and with his boyish imagination, thinking of all manner of reasons to their meaning and why or who had put them there. In fact, he had not been unlike Patrick and Joshua, with his interest in ancient history. Although he could not remember these visits at the time that Patrick and Joshua had first arrived in Atbara, it had sparked his curiosity or perhaps evoked old memories buried deep and long forgotten. He had found out that Joshua had visited these caves and it aroused his interest profoundly and combined with the mysterious woman in the coffee booth, that's what had initiated his visit to the caves, although he had not gone inside and then his visit to the coffee booth where he had finally met Evia. He was so glad that he had made that visit and shuddered at the thought of what would have happened to him had he not gone there. Before when he had tried to go to the cave, that weakness and nausea he had always felt as he approached had been so strong and unbearable that he had only managed to get within a few feet of its entrance and that was with a great effort, such was its force. The properties within the cave blocked off all signals and he realised that this was the cause of his problems. Being so dependent on T.R.I.G.O.M., the signals flowing through his body like his life's blood, grew weaker and weaker the nearer he got to the cave causing his weakness. Now that he was heading once again for the cave, he started to feel a little apprehensive, a fear growing inside him that he could not shake off. He tried to hide his anguish from the rest of them. He didn't want them to worry as they already had more than enough to concern themselves about. He could only hope that now he had become independent and free from control he would be able to enter the cave without any repercussions. The storm was growing fiercer by the minute and there was certainly no time to divert to anywhere else that could provide them shelter. Megan was still recovering from her ordeal and as he looked over at Patrick, he realised that all the recent events were taking their toll on him. He looked tired and pale. His usual jovial self, lost for the time being, taken over by a sadness and a constant look of worry. Patrick managed to smile at him briefly as he caught him looking. Braedan too began to feel sadness, but he quickly shook himself out of his negative thoughts; he was determined to get them all to safety. He directed all his energies to concentrating on driving and keeping control of the old car, which was getting harder by the minute even with his strength. Outside, the air had a red glow and as the lightning grew stronger, the whole of the car shook with its force. Braedan had to quickly manoeuvre through the disturbance that it left in its wake. The air rushing in to fill the vacuum that the lightning had created caused such a loud rumble of thunder that the car shook and Braedan only just managed to regain control. Patrick and Megan remained silent, allowing Braedan full concentration on the task at hand, frightened that if they spoke he would lose control and they would all be lost. Patrick breathed a sigh of relief as he managed to make out the cave coming up quickly before them, just in time as the old road came to a complete stop and the strain on the car had become too much; its engine losing its struggle for life. A bolt of lightning struck an old tree just a few yards from where they had stopped. The brilliance from its light was so strong that even Braedan had to close his eyes. They needed to get out and into safety urgently. Patrick and Megan had no idea of the fear that Braedan was now facing. Could he enter the cave or would he be unable to find safety within the sanctuary that it offered? He had no choice, he must try.

Chapter Fifty-Five

"Quick, come on, Braedan, we must get to the cave and get inside and hopefully the storm will pass soon. You can fill us in as to what has been happening when we are safe." The lightning flashed again, lighting up the whole of the car. They heard a soft sizzling noise and Patrick looked at Braedan in panic.

"I think that struck the car. Come on we need to move." Braedan quickly composed himself and helped Patrick free Megan from her seat. The passenger door would not open, for some reason it had become stuck. Braedan struggled. Even though his strength was far greater than the average human being, it took him some time before the door even started to move. Patrick helped him and with their joint strength managed to open the door just enough for Megan to get out. He beckoned to Megan and as she squeezed through the door she fell safely into his awaiting arms. She clung to him for a moment wanting the feeling of safety that she felt in his arms to last. He kissed her cheek tenderly before setting her down gently. The smell of burning was stronger now and so the urgency to get away from the car was becoming paramount. He looked up and beckoned to Braedan to signal him to move fast. Braedan's metallic skin was protecting him from the heat of the burning car as he pushed it clear of them all but he knew they had to hurry. He had no time to carefully step through the old shrubbery which surrounded them and in his haste his foot got tangled up in an old root which he had not seen. He shouted out loudly as he twisted his foot landing with a hard thud on the floor. He rolled over to his side and lay still. Patrick quickly ran over to him afraid that he was injured but he need not have worried, he was just shocked at the pain he had experienced in this foot. He was not used to having no control over the stability of his body. Patrick held out his hand to help him up and Braedan gladly accepted; overwhelmed by this gesture, this friendship and love for his sister that he now felt. Not even as a boy did he remember being a part of anything and certainly not a family. Yes he felt like they were now his family. All these new emotions were becoming too much for him and he slumped back down to the floor, causing Patrick to be concerned again. The flames were angrily shooting out of the car; it could explode at any minute. He knew it would not be long before the car was completely consumed by the flames and as the wind was getting stronger they needed to move now. Their lives were in danger.

"Can you get up?" Patrick had to shout to Braedan as the wind howled around them. He nodded and shakily got to his feet. Patrick put one arm around Megan and the other around Braedan as they started to head, as fast as they could, towards the cave. Braedan got slower and slower, feeling the effect of the cave on his body. He wasn't sure if it was psychological due to his past experiences or if it was real. However the nausea was not there but he could still sense a force as he got closer which surrounded his body, slowing him down. "You OK?" Patrick asked, once again concerned for him.

"Yes I will be OK. Just help me get to the cave and I will explain." He sounded almost breathless, struggling to breathe. Battling against the wind and storm they finally got to the mouth of the cave. Patrick and Megan moved quickly through its entrance to the safety within but Braedan stopped still. It seemed he was unable to move. Patrick instinctively held out his hand. Slowly Braedan moved his hand to touch that of his friends and within that moment, his strength returned. He had been welcomed in and was not afraid anymore.

Chapter Fifty-Six

They were inside the cave, safe from the raging storm outside. Who knew what havoc and damage was in its wake? Those unsuspecting people cocooned in their own Avatar worlds, not having any chance to flee its path or possessing the knowledge of the changes that it was bringing. This would only mark the start. The cave was not dark as Braedan had expected; it seemed to have its own light source. He marvelled that he felt so well. He could breathe and the strange force that he could sense seemed to be energising him. Patrick looked over at him with a puzzled look. Braedan smiled and explained to him, as briefly as he could, about his past experience of this cave. They had all sat on a large ledge, which ran the length of the wall where the largest of the symbols were etched into the cave above them. It was comfortable and warm and the ledge was just perfect to rest on. They hadn't noticed but Megan had wandered off whilst Braedan had been relating his story about the cave to Patrick and so they were surprised as they looked up to see her in front of them. She had in her hand a small flat stone on which she had piled up berries and fruit she had found in another part of the cave. Patrick hadn't realised just how hungry he was and couldn't even remember the last time he had eaten. Megan smiled. "It's OK, these are natural fruits, there is a small area through there," and she pointed to a passageway leading into what looked like another chamber. "It has water and food. They are all good to eat, look," and she immediately took a bite into a large yellow berry. "Mmmmm." She laughed, encouraging them to eat. Patrick needed no such encouragement and quickly took a handful, which he promptly devoured, he was so hungry. They tasted so good and he couldn't remember ever tasting anything so delicious. Megan turned to Braedan and offered him the slab of fruit.

"I am not sure if I can still eat anything solid. I have only been used to the protein substance that I have been fed by T.R.I.G.O.M.

She smiled at him. "Try, as you will need to be able to eat. It will be fine." Reassured by her warmth and generosity he picked up one of the smaller berries from the slab and held it to his nose. He was like a child being offered a sweet for the first time. Its smell was invigorating. He had nothing to compare it with, a strong sweet smell that compelled him to put it into his mouth. It was an explosion of flavours, his eyes wide with wonder as he savoured the sensation of its texture in his mouth. He began to chew, releasing more of its sweetness into his dry mouth. As he swallowed he closed his eyes, wanting to fully enjoy this wondrous experience. The juices from the fruit reviving taste buds he had not known he had possessed. He swallowed the fruit, his mouth completely refreshed, the taste still lingering in his mouth making him want more.

He felt the fruit slipping down his throat and it felt so good. "Mmmmm," he heard himself mutter. He opened his eyes to find Patrick and Megan smiling at him, so taken by his innocence with a tinge of sadness that he had lost so much. He smiled back at them, a little apprehensive that the fruit would have some sort of effect on his body, not having had solid food for such a long time. His worries were needless, indeed he felt better than ever, his energy had been restored and he felt, yes he felt happy.

Megan looked at them both. "I think we should take a drink too and then we can rest. Come follow me." She started towards the chamber that she had pointed out earlier. They eagerly followed, intrigued to see this source of food and water for themselves. The passageway was dark compared to where they had been sat in the entrance to the cave but as they passed through the chamber, it grew lighter and opened out into a bright underground oasis. A stream flowed through its centre and on each side of the stream there were rows and rows of berry-like plants of all different colours. They had never seen anything quite like it before. They could not see where the light was emanating from and although it was bright, it was a soft relaxing light, unlike the harsh glare of sunlight in the outside world. Megan walked to the flowing water and cupped her hand to catch some of it.

"Wait," Patrick shouted, but she had taken a drink and was smiling.

"It's OK, it's safe. I am not sure how I know but I do and I have already tasted the water on my first visit. It is cold and refreshing. Come, try some."

Both Patrick and Braedan drank the water. Immediately they started feeling refreshed. It was clear and cold, quenching their thirst and just like the berries, they felt the energy being restored to their bodies as they drank. The air inside this chamber felt fresh and cool; they had not felt so good for a long time. It was only here that they realised how polluted the outside air had become. They took deep long breaths, enjoying this feeling of well-being. They didn't need to speak, each one of them lost in their own thoughts, embracing this peace and the calmness of their surroundings. They had sat down by the flowing water. Megan had snuggled up to Patrick and Braedan sat opposite them. Patrick broke the tranquillity first. "Perhaps it's time to tell us what happened during our absence." Braedan nodded.

Chapter Fifty-Seven

Braedan began … It is exactly a month ago today since I saw you disappearing in the Air Disc. The pyramid and its surroundings had changed, the waters had evaporated and we were all in a state of confusion. T.R.I.G.O.M. had never experienced anything like it, I have never experienced such confusion. I thought that we could cope with anything. The usual signals which T.R.I.G.O.M. used to instruct and control had become distorted sending out confusing messages to myself and the Hubots alike. As the signals grew weaker and weaker, the Hubots were unable to function, most of them just collapsing where they stood. This, however, was not the case for me. I started to regain control over my thoughts and actions even though I was still receiving partial signals from T.R.I.G.O.M. I had become stronger and knew that I was now my own person, my own being who would never be controlled again. I had evolved again and had passed the point of needing T.R.I.G.O.M. or its Council. For me it was a poignant moment of realisation and, in a strange way, it marked the rebirth of my soul. Although I can't fully explain this to you, it was as if another force had taken over, something more powerful and wonderful than any man-made computer could create. I stood relishing this moment, not full of anger and hatred but full of joy and hope, but above all else full of a love of life and a life to come. I looked over at the pyramid, its pulsating vibrations reaching out to me. Its energy touching my very being, it was as though it were healing me with its life giving powers. It looked so beautiful, majestic in its presence and everything around it blossomed with life. Then I noticed that the door that had been opened was now shut. It had started to fade from this wonderful creation back to its faded façade. As its vibrations faded, I could still feel its force within me, feeling no fear that it was changing, just calmness and a deep feeling that all was as it should be. I instantly knew that I should go and as I turned to walk away, the waters were slowly starting to return. I quickened my pace, not wanting to be stranded, the water was rapidly rising. The bodies of the fallen Hubots were being swallowed up by the returning water, there was nothing that I could do for them, they were not part of the future plan of that I was certain in my own mind. Your friends were safe within the pyramid, for what purpose I did not know but I knew that this was their destiny and I had no power to change or intervene. I began to run, running for longer than I could remember, not daring to turn around. I could feel the vibrations, but its force was growing weaker, its pulses grew less and less. It was only when they had stopped completely that I allowed myself to stop and turn to look.

I was amazed at what I saw. It was like nothing had ever happened. The old pyramid stood, looking old and crumbling once again, its beauty and purpose concealed from this world. The water had now consumed the Hubots, their lifeless bodies hidden in its depths. All that could be heard was the gentle lapping of the water as it caressed the sides of the pyramid. The storm had passed over for the time being and everything was calm and eerily still. Not a breeze or the usual hum of machinery, the connection to T.R.I.G.O.M. had not been restored. I had expected the connection to return as soon as everything had returned to normal. I felt a sudden loss, I was alone. After all even if a mother who is uncaring, a child will always miss her when she is not there and T.R.I.G.O.M. had once been all I had, a Mother and a Father. Although it had taken away so much it had also given me new life. I started to feel this new found energy slowly ebbing away and it was at this moment that I saw one of those coffee booths in the distance. I knew that it had not been there before but from my past experience I saw it as a welcome sign, a shelter from harm and so I headed towards it. As I got closer, I saw Evia waiting at the doorway, waving me to come in. The air remained still; it felt like time itself had stopped. I almost fell inside the door, such was my relief to see a friendly face. I was so in need of comfort, I felt so alone and confused. Evia smiled at me, her usual knowing smile and pointed to a chair near to the coffee counter and into which I thankfully sank into. As I fell into the chair, closing my eyes, feeling so tired with all the past events, I felt Evia's hand on mine. It had been a long time since I had felt such tenderness, her small tactile gesture had made me feel so happy but at the same time it had not reached the sadness of my soul. She sensed my feelings, in that special way she does and told me that I would be fine and that my sadness would go in time. She made me feel like I had a purpose, she gave me hope for the future and that we still had time left to live and learn. She told me that you would return to this place and gave me the time and date to be here to meet you. I didn't even question how she would know or the hows or whys. I knew there would be no point, I just trusted in her information. She had given me a large cup of coffee whilst she had been talking to me and now as I drank this wonderful tasting coffee, the likes that I had never tasted before, I felt at peace. I don't know what was in it, but it reached every part of me and seemed to heal all those insecurities; the sadness I had felt so deep inside of me. I wanted to stay there forever, safe in this time bubble of peace.

Chapter Fifty-Eight

I had stayed for what seemed hours, just drinking and sitting in the serene surroundings, my energy returning to me, my whole being energised in readiness for whatever I had to face. Eventually, after finishing my coffee, I smiled at Evia and got up from my seat. She had told me a lot, but some things were meant for only me and so they will remain with me. I knew where I was heading to and turned to kiss her goodbye. She hugged me with so much love that I actually felt tears in my eyes. I had a strange feeling that I would not see her again, so I hugged her tightly before walking through the door, back to the outside world. I started to walk away from the coffee booth and after a few yards felt a slight tremor under my feet, I turned around to look back at the coffee booth, but it was gone and yet I was not surprised. I smiled as I turned to carry on my journey. I had still not received any signals from T.R.I.G.O.M. and so I headed towards Atbara, a journey on foot that took me along the Nile on to a path that I had never taken before. Wildlife still existed, even though it was in a small minority. It gave me time to reflect and I wondered at these creatures and plants that they had such strength and the will to survive. They had battled through extreme weather conditions, surviving all the odds, outwitting T.R.I.G.O.M. and its culture who had actively tried to control nature and its inhabitants. I was seeing life as I walked, like I had never seen before, I had never been interested in the world as it was, only as T.R.I.G.O.M. had wanted it to be. It was now around evening time and the light was just starting to fade as I walked. Although I had covered some distance, I knew that I would not reach Atbara before nightfall, so I started to look for some shelter. The sky still had that strange red glow and I could see the moon through the grey clouds. It was larger than I could remember, it seemed so close and it looked like it had a halo of light around it. It looked quite eerie and again everything seemed so still. Quite unexpectedly a loud hooting noise broke the silence of my thoughts, making me jump with surprise. I had reached a large tree, it looked so old. Oh what times it must have seen if only it could relate its stories. I heard the noise again and it was very loud so I knew its source must be very close to me. A rustle in the tree made me look up and there blinking at me was a large bird. I drew closer, it was the most beautiful owl I had ever seen. Although only having seen them from a computer generated image, I was taken aback by its size and its beauty. I felt no fear from this bird that showed no fear at my presence either. I don't know what possessed me to do it but I impulsively held out my arm. It looked at me for a few seconds with those unblinking eyes, not in any rush to move and then swiftly and gracefully outstretched its wings and flew towards me landing deftly on my outstretched arm, its head turning almost full circle to look straight at me. I stood completely still, not daring to move in case it should fly away. I wanted its company as crazy as that sounds. I was not afraid of being alone but I felt reassured by this creature although I didn't know why. It called out into the night again, its sound breaking the silence as it flapped its wings to take off but it only flew a short distance to the right and then returned to my arm. I instinctively knew it wanted me to follow it. I wasted no time and without hesitation started to walk in the direction that it had flown. We seemed to be heading towards the edge of the Nile, where the water was lapping gently against the bank. There was a small clearing which was well sheltered with large bushes and trees. The view of the Nile was stunning, the moon's reflection lighting up the water sparkling like stars on its surface. It almost took my breath away with the beauty of this place. The owl left my arm and perched on a low branch looking out over the water so I sat down beside it and looked around me. Why had mankind always been controlled by selfishness and greed? These tendencies only lead them to destroy many of nature's own provisions on their quest for a better world and a greater knowledge of all things. The ironic sadness of this was that this wonderful planet had already provided them with everything they needed and all that was required for anything better was for them to look to their inner selves, to cherish their own kind and nature's precious gifts. I knew that things were changing in the skies, the universal changes would mean adaption again to the dwellers of the Earth and for which I would play some part. My recreation had perhaps not been in vain, even intentional and for a purpose. My thoughts turned to Joshua and Torri. They were safe and their future was beyond this time and place, preparing for the time that I could not even imagine. A shiver ran through me. I knew I had to get back to the T.R.I.G.O.M. headquarters and see what had happened or what needed to be done. I would set off at first light, my plans were made. For now though, I lay back on the grass and digested more of the magical views this place had to offer. My eyes began to close with the serenity of this place and the hypnotic lapping of the water.

Chapter Fifty-Nine

The night air had turned cool, the moon glowed red in the night sky, but as I lay trying to get some rest, my sensors detected a strong light and it wasn't the moon, although that seemed brighter than usual. I looked up over the water and noticed strange rings of light forming on the water's surface which were growing brighter by the second. I think that my new friend the owl had been disturbed by the distant rumbles of thunder and the brightness of the light as it suddenly took flight and headed off into the night air, leaving me alone. The light so strong now that it lit up the whole surrounding area, just as bright as daylight. I think my poor owl friend must have been very confused. Up until that point I had been having strange thoughts of old times where druids practised their magic by moonlight, birds being used as messengers to warn of impending danger, old stories of Camelot and Merlin teaching his magic, appearing as an owl to teach his master the old arts. So many strange thoughts had been swirling about in my head. The moon falling from the sky crashing into the water made me physically jump and the metal parts of my body actually felt heavier than usual as I sat bolt upright. Realising, thankfully, that I must have been dreaming, I began to focus on the reality of my surroundings. I felt quite lonely without my companion but the rings of light now distracted me from my thoughts and so I stood up slowly, moving closer to the water's edge to investigate this light source. Although I have highly advanced neural optical vision giving me so much more information than the normal human eye, this light was different and I was finding it difficult to process. Then, as I stood and watched, gradually I could make out what appeared to be small symbols glowing within the light itself, almost like they were dancing around the ring of light. I didn't feel afraid, just enthralled as to what it might mean. My part human, part computer brain started to analyse the symbols that I could make out. It was a DNA code I was sure of it. I have been able to store the symbols to memory, sensing that this was important to do so. The lights were getting dimmer as the moon's light had started to give way to the rising sun and it would soon be time for my journey to continue. I knew that the symbols were important, I had them stored away feeling that was the reason that they had appeared to me. There was no sign of the owl that had kept me company partially through the night and to whom I seemed to have formed an unspoken friendship but as I set off again, I heard the hoot of an owl in the distance which made me smile; my friend was still there somewhere watching over me. My task was to get back to base, but I had not seen any signs of any drones patrolling the area, I had no link with the computer main frame and more strangely I had not seen any people or transport as I neared the main city. I began to feel weary, I had not had any sustenance for some time and although I can go for long periods without anything, my body was telling me it needed my usual shot of proteins which I could get when I got back to base. The roads were too quiet and the silence was deafening; I needed to hurry and find out what had happened. I neared the base and along the way I passed a handful of dwelling cells and as there seemed to be no activity I could not resist but to investigate. I walked up to the first one, which was a small cell, usually only occupied by one person and stopped at the door. Normally my presence would have generated a welcome and an I.D. probe, but there was nothing. I instinctively pushed the door, which opened with ease. I was shocked, it should not have let me in without DNA authorisation. I stepped through the door. It looked like most every cell dwelling looked, the occasional person adding personal touches but as most people were not interested in that sort of thing, they tended to all look identical and clinical. I looked over to the sitting quarters, the place where the computer linked its occupant to the Avatar worlds which were growing ever more popular. I gasped, the occupant was sat in her moulded chair, linked to the computer but there appeared to be no sign of life. She looked in her middle to late twenties with a mass of golden hair. The chair which should have kept her secure had failed and her hair had fallen over her face as her body had slumped forward. It struck me how beautiful she was and how alone she looked.

I was intrigued and then it occurred to me that the vibration and signals that the pyramid had given off must have somehow frozen everything and anyone who had been linked to the computer was more than likely still locked within it. I reached down to feel for a pulse, her skin felt warm and I could feel a very faint pulse. I was so relieved but knew I had to work quickly to set her free and wondered how many others must be in the same situation. I had to get to T.R.I.G.O.M. I was part of the system that had created isolation, encouraged less physical interaction. I felt ashamed and saddened. What had the human race become? I gently sat her back in her chair, telling her that I was going to take her with me and that I would help. I am not sure if she heard me but I wasn't going to let her down. Holding her hand, my sensors detected her identification chip and so I was instantly able to get her information. Her name was Olivia. Such a lovely name, I whispered to her, her body limp but at least she was alive. Ensuring that she was disconnected from the computer links that she had been attached to, I scooped her up into my arms and stepped back through the door and back into the deserted streets.

Chapter Sixty

Although I had calculated that it must have been around mid-day by now, it was still quite dark. The sun was up but it was hardly penetrating the thick cloud that had formed overhead. I actually shivered not through the cold but the bleakness I felt surrounding me. I set off in the direction of the base, I hadn't got far to go now. My pace quickening in my urgency to see what damage had been sustained by T.R.I.G.O.M. I approached its headquarters with caution and as I walked through its extensive grounds the eerie silence overwhelmed me. The large gates were slightly ajar as I pushed them to open them so that I could get through safely. I was still holding Olivia tightly in my arms as I walked carefully through. I could not sense any signals at all or detect any activity as I walked up to the main doors. The strong vibrations and energy surge from the pyramid must have been something so powerful, far beyond the capabilities of T.R.I.G.O.M. Nothing seemed to be working and as I walked into the main lobby, I saw Drones and Hubots collapsed everywhere. Drones, unlike some of the Hubots were completely artificial life forms and could only function completely through commands from their controller. I had never seen anything like it before, I was beginning to panic. Everything was different, my world turned upside down. I laid Olivia down on one of the seats in the reception area, I needed to think and assess the situation. I looked around and saw one of the X class Hubots slumped in the far corner. These Hubots were different in the fact that they were not totally reliant on function commands. They still had an element of Human capability, however this one seemed unable to move and it looked like its leg had been damaged. As I approached its eyes focused on me; its light was very faint but I could sense its fear and confusion. Its light faded a little as it recognised me, I could only touch it as reassurance knowing I had to see T.R.I.G.O.M. before I could help anything or anyone. The place was in total darkness but I knew this place inside out and didn't need the use of directional lights or transportation aides. I passed the tubes, not stopping to look at anything else. I ran through the long corridors, ascending down to the depths, to the heart of T.R.I.G.O.M. As I drew closer I felt a tingling sensation through my body and a faint buzzing in my head. If it was a signal it was far too weak for me to decipher. Was it a cry for help? It was compelling me to run faster; I could feel the urgency. At last I entered the cool room within the depths of the building and before me was the great T.R.I.G.O.M. dark and almost silent. Only a very faint intermittent buzzing noise broke the silence of the room. I gasped. Never would I have thought that anything could destroy or incapacitate this once all powerful creation. At this point I was unsure to the extent of the damage so I moved closer to inspect its Central Processing Unit. I touched its heart. Within that moment I felt a power surging through me. I couldn't move, but within that split second I felt its need to survive, wanting its power to be part of me. I was stronger. It had created me but I was now the master of it and I had to sever its links so that humanity could once again be free. The chips in each human had allowed T.R.I.G.O.M. to control them and as it was now paralysed so too was everything it was connected to; the only exception was me. As I let go, I felt its hopelessness and desperation. Did this machine have a soul? I had no time to ponder on such an idea, there was a louder buzzing before its light faded completely. There was an air of death, of loss, causing me to hesitate, this after all had once been everything to me, Mother, Father and provider. With a shaking hand and a heavy heart, I did what I had to do and T.R.I.G.O.M. was no more. The last bit of its power ebbed away. It was dying as I watched and so its control on all those Avatar worlds died, with it releasing its captives. I could not move with the mixed feelings of grief and release that I felt. It was only when I heard a noise coming from behind me that I eventually moved. I turned around to see what the source of this noise was. It was one of the Hubots. It was looking at me, holding up its arms but not able to move. I rushed over to it. It was trying to speak but it was so weak it could not form the words. I knew the Hubots could be saved but I would have to work hard to ensure that they survived without the force that they had been linked to and had come to depend upon. I suddenly remembered Olivia. Was she alright? I quickly retraced my steps to the upper levels and finally got back to the main reception area, where I had left her. There she was just starting to regain consciousness looking bewildered and frightened. She didn't know me so I was careful in my approach to her but she didn't seem to care who I was she just held on to me needing comfort and holding her I didn't feel alone and I realised that I had a lot to do but did not want to be alone again.

Chapter Sixty-One

Patrick and Megan listened intently to Braedan as he carried on to tell them how he had gathered as many Hubots together as he could, making any minor repairs that could be done manually to their systems in order for them to function even to a basic level. Outside, it was still calm and although it should have been daylight it was so dark, nothing moved and the air was thick. Whatever change was going to happen was coming soon, he had to be quick. Braedan continued. "I sent the Hubots back towards the town to gather as many people as possible with instructions to head for the caves. I needed to come and get you and now that you are safe here I must return. I need to get Olivia and bring as many people as possible to the safety of the local caves and hills, just away from the main town and the danger of collapsing buildings. She wanted to stay with the Hubots to help so I must now go and make sure she is alright. I will return to you here, as soon as I can. This cave is perfect, I should have thought of it before but there are many scattered about which will hopefully protect and save as many people as possible."

Patrick saw the urgency in his eyes, he felt his compassion and wanted to help but he knew that for some reason he needed to stay here with Megan and that Braedan was much better prepared to cope with the elements outside. He didn't want to slow him down so he nodded his understanding and gave him a hug; no words were needed. Megan too understood and hugged him tightly before he set off. Looking back only once, Braedan headed towards the cave's entrance and as another flash of lightning struck, he was gone. They could only hope that he would be safe. Patrick and Megan stood for some time looking out through the cave's entrance, half expecting Braedan to reappear.

"Come." Patrick turned to Megan. "Let us get some rest, we can rest over there." He pointed to a soft piece of soil that had a few leaves scattered on it just the other side of the cave's entrance. "We need to rest and gather our strength for when Braedan returns."

Megan nodded, they were both tired and she put up no resistance as she snuggled into him. Patrick closed his eyes and even though he was exhausted, sleep would not come. Instead he just rested letting his mind wander and ponder over all that had happened. He looked around the cave and remembered the stories of early cave men. Was it possible that something similar had happened before and these caves had provided sanctuary until the day that man could once again step outside into a changed world? Perhaps seeming primitive to a world in which man had to adapt again and evolve? It was as he was imagining what it must have been like looking out from a cave for the first time and seeing a strange new world, that he gradually succumbed to the peace of sleep. With Megan's arms tightly around him, he relaxed and for the first time in such a long time, he rested, his limbs losing their aches and pains as his body relaxed and the tension eased. It had been like he had been living on adrenalin for so long and now his wandering thoughts abated as finally he slept effortlessly, floating in and out of dreams. Wonderful dreams of carefree days when the sun was shining bright in the sky. He was free to drive his car. The road was long and straight, full of trees and the air so fresh. He could hear birds singing in their branches, such an abundance of wildlife, it was nature in all its glory. The sky was full of different colours so vibrant above him. He didn't find it strange that the sky was not blue; it was normal now. It made him feel so full of life, of hope and yes, even excitement which he wanted to last forever. A violent rumble of thunder, which vibrated through the cave, tore Patrick away from his dreams. He opened his eyes and quickly looked at Megan, she was still sleeping soundly. He was glad that she had not been disturbed and also a little jealous of her ability to sleep so soundly. He was about to try and find that beautiful dream place again when he thought he saw a shadow appear at the other end of the cave where they had eaten and drunk from earlier. He slowly unfolded Megan's arms from around his body, being very careful to not disturb her. This done he quietly got up and walked slowly, being careful not to make a noise, in the direction of the shadow. He could hear only his heart beating now, he was sure that any minute his heart was going to pound out of his chest but he slowly moved forward. The cave was brighter towards the entrance to the stream and his eyes gradually began to focus. He noticed a large stick laying slightly to the right of him and so he bent down to pick it up. "Maybe he might need it," he thought. It seemed to give him a little more courage, his heart still pumping wildly in his chest, hardly daring to breathe.

Chapter Sixty-Two

Braedan battled against the strong wind and driving rain. He knew that this was just a drop in the ocean for what was to come and that he needed to hurry. Even his strengthened body struggled to move forward with the force of the wind. He had a way to go, yet he had to keep going. The ground beneath him trembled from a distant earthquake. He tried to go faster. He was out in the open, there was no escaping the pounding rain that made a strange pinging sound as it pounded against the metallic parts of his body. It was hard to see anything clearly in front of him, he just aimed his body and carried on. Then, through the noise of the storm, he heard a different sound which made him stop for a moment to listen. He could hardly believe what he heard, yes it sounded like a hoot of an owl and even through the howling winds and deafening thunder, he could make out its distinguishing calls. It was like a melody suddenly cutting through a jumble of sounds. It appeared to be coming from somewhere to his left and so he turned towards it. He hadn't noticed before but there was a large tree just a few feet away from him, he headed towards it. Its long branches provided a little respite from the battering winds enough for him to be able to focus more clearly on his surroundings. The owl cried out again and he changed his direction again to head towards it. Beyond the tree was a small dirt track, clearly not used very often but still he could make it out. It seem to lead downwards and had small bushes alongside of it. The urgent cry of the owl again urged him to head towards it. The path led down beyond the surface of the harsh terrain above him. The bushes that seemed so small gave him protection as he went downwards. He knew that he was heading in the right direction and this path enabled him to move faster and gave him significant shelter to be able to continue his journey. He would never have realised that this path existed if he hadn't heard the owl. He smiled to himself; his friend was still watching over him. He still couldn't see the owl but he felt its presence. With not so much wind force, he was able to move faster. He wanted to get back to Olivia and make sure that she was safe. Why had he not brought her with him to meet Patrick and Megan? He had thought she would be safer within the T.R.I.G.O.M. head-quarters as she wanted to stay and help but on reflection now, he realised that the caves were probably the only form of protection that any of them would get. The path was narrow and mud-dy, in some parts he found it hard to lift his feet but his strength persevered and held out. His head was just below the surface of the ground, small bushes shielding him further from the strong winds. He could smell the earth, something which he had never experienced before; he wondered how long this trench had been here. It looked quite new and it intrigued him as to how and why it should be here. It appeared to be straight with no wind-ing curves which made him think that it had been intention-ally created by someone. These casual thoughts eased the pan-ic that had been growing inside him. He hadn't stopped to rest letting his imagination distract him with the mystery trench as the weather worsened above him. Eventually the trench became even narrower as the path started upwards again before it came to an end. His head was now above ground level as he continued walking upwards, and then he was back on the surface, feeling the wind's full force once again. As he looked around to get his bearings, he recognised this terrain and he knew he was close to the T.R.I.G.O.M. headquarters. Still battling against the wind, he eventually could make out some shapes in the distance but he didn't recognise them. He should have reached the T.R.I.G.O.M. building by now but he could only make out odd shapes which were less than a couple of hundred yards before him. He stopped to focus and stared in amazement. The familiar sight of the building that he was expecting to see was not there. Part of the building still stood but the main structure of the building had crumbled, its debris scattered and a large crater stood in his path. Earth-quakes were happening all over but this took him completely by surprise, the panic rising up inside him. He had left Olivia here. His heart pounded as he tried to manoeuvre around the crater to reach the shell of the building. Debris was scattered all around, parts of metal strewn across the ground. He felt sick. The back part of the building still remained relatively intact. He headed towards it as fast as he could. He screamed out aloud, "Please let her be alive." He didn't know who he was screaming to but for the first time, he felt there was more than what he could see or compute and whatever or whoever it was, he felt every fibre of his being reaching out to find Olivia alive.

Chapter Sixty-Three

Clutching the stick tightly, his knuckles almost white, Patrick approached the doorway where he had seen the shadow. Trying to move quietly he drew nearer, he had almost stopped breathing with fear. With the stick out in front of him, more to give him courage than protection, he moved very slowly forward then suddenly a hand grabbed his wrist so that the stick could do no damage.

"It's OK, Patrick, it's me." The familiar voice like music to his ears, Patrick let out a long gasp of breath which he had been holding in, his heart still pounding.

"Oh my God, you frightened me to death and you nearly got this stick over your head."

Admar smiled. "No I don't think that there was any fear of that." Admar was laughing. Patrick too found himself laughing and it occurred to him that he had never heard Admar laugh before. It was infectious and calming, making Patrick almost forget where he was and the circumstances that had befallen them all. Megan woke from her sleep, wondering what the noise was and Patrick smiling at Admar went over to her to reassure her that everything was alright. Admar beckoned them both to follow him through the passage to where the stream flowed and where the light was better. This place is so tranquil, thought Patrick as he looked around. They sat by the stream's edge and Admar turned to them both. "I have come to say goodbye." Patrick's smile vanished in an instant. Evia appeared through another passageway which Patrick had not noticed before and took Admar's hand. Looking at them both, Patrick thought how young they looked now a halo of light silhouetted around their bodies, both looking so peaceful but also sad. Evia turned to the passageway from which she had come and as she did so Patrick followed her gaze. Once again he thought he saw shadows in the distance and as he stared, the shadows took form. Patrick's mouth dropped open in surprise, the shadows becoming more solid as they drew closer. Then his smile returned as he shouted out, "Josh, Torri."

Megan, who had been standing close to Patrick, also jumped and let out a loud gasp as she recognised her old school friend. She could not contain herself, she let go of Patrick and ran towards Torri, who in turn held out her arms to embrace her old friend. Patrick smiled. So they had known each other. He watched them hug each other, he too wasted no time and followed suit by running up to Josh and hugging him tightly, afraid to let go just in case he should disappear. Patrick could hear Josh laughing as Patrick still clung to him.

"It's OK, my old friend and it's so good to see you," Josh said breathlessly, having been squeezed so hard by Patrick he was pretending to be struggling for breath.

"I never thought I was going to see you again," Patrick stuttered. He was trying hard to keep the tears from his eyes. All his emotions welling up inside, he needed release and turned away. He could not control his tears.

Josh put his arm on his shoulders. "It's OK, my friend. We have all been through such a lot and we will all have to adjust to what we have deemed our fate."

Admar and Evia now beckoned to Torri and Joshua. They did not have long to stay so their time was precious. Torri turned to Patrick and Megan. "We will see you again but you will sleep for a long time, here where you will be protected. When Braedan returns he will have the genetic code that you will need to survive this current apocalypse and when the time is right you will emerge with Braedan to inhabit your new home, although you will not remember this life. Your bodies will be made compatible in order for you to live in the new world as you have done before, as we all have done before. This time though it will not just be changing of cultures but a changing of the world's form. Josh and I will be here to help and guide as Admar and Evia have been for so many centuries. The Pyramid of Life will protect the

Earth for some time yet before its transformation, but eventually a new world, new life will begin."

Patrick looked puzzled and looked at Admar. Admar took Patrick to one side and spoke quietly. "I will do this one last thing for you so that you know that all will be well. Close your eyes, Patrick and I will restore one of your old memories so that you will remember and understand."

Patrick closed his eyes.

Chapter Sixty-Four

Braedan raced towards the remains of the building, shouting out her name. "OLIVIA."

He spotted one of the Hubots partly covered with rubble. He rushed over to it, frantically trying to clear some of the heavy debris that was pinning it to the floor. Braedan recognised this Hubot, it was one of the luckier ones that he had restored to minimal functions and one that he had left Olivia with. He spoke urgently to it, as he managed to get it free from the final stone that had trapped it. "Where is she? Is she safe?"

The Hubot could only manage a few broken words in its monotone vocabulary. "Data incomplete, data incomplete." Braedan suddenly felt angry, pushing the Hubot to one side, angry that it could not give him the information he needed. The rain which had started off lightly had got faster, it was pounding on the metal body of the Hubot and looking down at this defenceless being, Braedan's anger towards it subsided. This artificial being was not to blame and he lifted its limp body up out of the rubble and set it down against part of a wall that was still standing, giving it partial protection from the unpredictable elements. After ensuring that the Hubot was safe, he headed into the remaining shell of the building. Just then a lightning bolt struck and the place lit up. There was a strong smell of burning and he called out her name again. The thunder roared; he couldn't hear anything except the roaring vacuum filling with air as another lightning bolt hit the building. He stumbled and was unable to stop himself from falling to the floor. He put out his arm to shield himself from the falling stones and debris. He didn't hit the floor lightly but managed to roll quickly out of the way of a piece of metal that missed him only by inches. As he lay on the ground trying to get his bearings again, the owl appeared before him landing on his outstretched arm. Amongst all the chaos, it looked at him calmly, its eyes blinking quickly, before it took flight. Braedan instinctively got up and started to follow it as it flew to the opposite side of the building. It was heading towards the entrance to where the main council used to attend their meetings. The owl landed briefly by one of the old Air Disc pads and then immediately took off again, disappearing from sight and leaving Braedan once again alone. He looked around quickly; he knew that his friend had brought him here for a reason. It was so dark now he had to scan the area using his night sensory vision. He noticed a large piece of metal in the far corner and went over to investigate. As he got closer he saw a small hand protruding from the side of the metal panel. He had no time to think and fearing the worst, he managed to push the metal to one side and there under it lay Olivia. She was so still, a large cut on her head with a trail of blood running down her cheek. He held his breath as he felt for a pulse. Yes there it was, just very faint but she was alive. The relief was overwhelming, he had no idea what injuries she had so before lifting her up he did a quick scan of her body. The head wound was not as bad as it first appeared and she had a few broken ribs, everything else seemed to be fine. He lifted her up into his arms, the burning smell now getting stronger. He started to run, retracing his steps back towards the track that had brought him here. He had just cleared the building, when the first explosion vented its force, almost knocking Braedan from his feet. The Hubot, whom he had helped earlier who had just managed to get to its feet, was once again knocked down, falling into Braedan's path and it was only by sheer luck he managed to avoid tumbling himself. Braedan gently put Olivia down so that he could help the Hubot back to its feet. He had no time now to check on any other survivors, he had to get back to the cave with Olivia. The Hubot now had a job to do. He quickly instructed the Hubot to head back to Atbara. "Gather as many people as you can find and head for the caves," he shouted at the Hubot, the roar of the flames caused by the explosion so loud now that he could hardly hear himself speak. The Hubot nodded its understanding and shakily turned around in the direction of the town. Braedan could feel the heat from the burning building, he scooped Olivia back up in his arms and started to run, retracing his steps back to the path. He had to return to the Cave of Symbols, to Patrick and Megan, it was crucial.

Chapter Sixty-Five

Patrick felt relaxed as he closed his eyes, listening to Admar's calming voice which filled his mind and then he could hear his voice no more, instead he was actually walking along a meadow clothed in a long white robe. He looked up at the clear blue sky, the sun's warmth flowing through his body making him feel alive and invigorated. The beautiful and enchanting coast of Kerry on his left, resplendent in all its glory as its sea captured the sun's rays with perfection. The light reflecting back as sparkles of light, almost blinding to the eyes. To his right, a mountainous terrain rising high into the skyline, yes the mountains, the caves they have always been there, throughout the history of the Earth, the history of man. He felt himself smiling. He knew that to the east lay County Limerick and to the South-East County Cork, places he had visited many times, through many lives. He smiled again as he remembered, he had lived here many centuries ago but this was more than just a memory he was experiencing, he was actually here in fifth century Ireland as the person he had once been. Patrick, a man of the cloth who had come to Ireland to spread knowledge and faith in these pagan times. His role here was important as his new role in the future would be and this particular life was being replayed back to him for a reason. It was a time when a new era was taking shape and his role was to teach, nurture and guide the Earth's children towards their future. He walked towards the mountains, the gentle waves lapping on the shoreline, the only sound in this peaceful place, his own bubble in time. He now remembered this life experience as he walked and with the help of Admar he recalled … He was 16 and it was not here in this beautiful part of Ireland where he dwelt but rather in England, where the climate was colder and the landscape less beautiful. His family, however, were not poor, as many were in this time but they had a flourishing estate, good clothes and always a full table of food to feed their hunger and he was well loved and looked after. He was not now in his safe bubble but actually in this time. He felt cold, his skin dirty, he wanted to still be walking in the sunshine clad in his white robe, and he shivered. It was a rainy day, late in the afternoon and he had been picking potatoes from the field for supper, lost in his own thoughts, when he heard loud shouts. He remembered seeing his father running towards him, waving his arms and shouting to him, but he couldn't make out his words at first. He saw and felt the panic in his father's eyes as he was frantically waving and shouting at him. Straining to hear his words, his father shouted louder, RUN, HIDE. Just before the darkness fell he saw the six men chasing his father, wielding swords and axes, their faces full of hatred and violence as they closed in on him. His father falling to the ground. He heard his mother's screams coming from the house. He didn't know which way to turn – to help his father or answer his mother's screams. His panic overwhelmed him until he could bear it no more. He turned to run but it was too late, the blow caught the side of his head, rendering him unconscious. He fell to the ground with a heavy thud. Looking at it now back in his white robe, viewing it as a third party back in his safe meadow where Admar had taken him, he could see the raiders clearly as they rampaged through his father's beloved estate. Irish slave traders had penetrated the defence wall, everywhere had to be protected in those days but it had been to no avail, they were everywhere and there were so many of them. They didn't care who they killed, they were looking for their bounty and Patrick was just one of their victims that day. Many others had fallen victim to these barbarians. As he watched he was glad that he could feel no pain, he was just observing, remembering as he looked on. His body had been bundled into a sack and was being dragged along the stony ground being battered and bruised where he was to join the pile of other bodies waiting on a nearby cart. There must have been another ten bodies at least all piled on to that old wooden cart. Some had regained consciousness and were shouting and screaming, only to be rewarded by a vicious kick from their enslavers, until they shouted no more and silence prevailed. Patrick remembered being frightened, his head throbbing from the vicious blow that he had received, hardly able to breathe in the heavy sack that held him prisoner. It smelt of blood and sweat. He wanted to be sick, the panic welling up inside him until thankfully he passed out again. Patrick could see all of this calmly now, being able to move at will in and out of physical, feeling all the emotions and pain that he had done at the time, all that time ago. He skipped over the long trek that it had taken to get to Ireland, the heartbreak, the physical pain that he had endured. He had full control with the help of Admar. He took a moment now to enjoy the fresh air of this time. It was not like the air of his current time. He had forgotten how fresh it was without the modern pollution which had seeped in over the years and the years of climate change. At first it had made him gasp as he took a deep breath to fill his lungs; the air was so pure. He had adapted without knowing to the sulphur taste and dense air so he enjoyed this moment of purity filling his lungs with it.

He could fast forward time, leaving out the parts that he didn't need to revisit, which brought him to his first introduction to the country that he eventually came to love and call his own, his beloved Ireland.

Chapter Sixty-Six

The boat had landed, the journey had been rough and some of the poor young victims had not survived. Their broken bodies had been casually discarded overboard, no one to grieve for them, no one to show compassion for their deaths, just cast into the ocean as waste, devoured by the dark seas to be consumed by the creatures within it. Patrick didn't know if he was thankful to still be alive or whether he would have preferred to have given in to death and ended his pain and suffering. Later, he would be thankful that he had survived but now he had landed in a strange place, not knowing his fate or why he had been brought here. His captors seemed to have no respect for human life; they were herded like cattle off the boat, hardly able to walk with the heavy shackles around their ankles. If they could not stand they were dragged and kicked until they were all on shore. Slave trading was big business in Ireland and many had suffered under the hands of these savage pirates. He was lying on his side, where he had been thrown, trying to catch his breath as the heavy landing had winded him and his ribs were sore. His stomach churned through hunger which was making him feel sick. At this moment he had wanted to die, his will to keep going deserting him.

"Get up, get up, and don't let them think you are weak or you will be no good to them." Patrick mustered up the energy to lift his head to see who this voice belonged to. He could barely see, the rain was falling so fast making it hard to open his eyes. The voice belonged to a boy, tall and skinny. He was covered in mud so it was hard to determine his age but Patrick thought he looked just a bit younger than himself. He had long black curly hair with large brown eyes which were looking down at Patrick with great concern through long black eyelashes. The boy offered Patrick his hand, which he took hesitantly, feeling the strength in his arm as he helped him to his feet. He smiled at him and instantly their friendship was formed.

"What are they going to do with us?" Patrick whispered. The boy knelt down and beckoned Patrick to do the same. He sniffed wiping his nose on his dirty arm, and drew Patrick closer to him.

"We are to be sold as slaves but only the strongest will survive, the weakest they kill." He emphasised this with an imaginary noose and actions of someone being hung, his tongue out and hanging to one side. This almost made Patrick laugh, his face was so comical but this was not time for laughter. Just then a girl approached them; they were to be given enough water and bread to keep them alive.

The boy turned to Patrick. "My name is Ferdy and her name is Florence. She will give you extra bread if you talk to her nicely." Patrick too, introduced himself quickly and Ferdy smiled at him, a cheeky smile, which Patrick marvelled at his bravery and the fact that he was able to keep his sense of humour under such circumstance. Patrick noticed a strange lilt in his voice which he had never heard before indicating that he was certainly not from anywhere he knew of.

"I have been here a few days so I have got to know a little about them." Ferdy pointed to their enslavers who had now gathered around a large fire, eating heartily and drinking large amounts of ale. As the ale flowed, their drunken banter was getting louder by the minute. Florence offered them bread and water, which they readily accepted. Patrick was so eager for the food that he had not noticed Florence secretly placing something else into Ferdy's hand. Patrick hungrily devouring the bread and guzzled down the water before anyone could take it away. Florence smiled at them both and Ferdy took her hand to try and place a cheeky kiss but she quickly pulled her hand away looking over worriedly to the men to make sure that they had not been seen. She knelt down and whispered something into Ferdy's ear. He nodded and she quickly got up to leave.

"Oi, you wench." One of the men was looking over at her and shouted, "Come here if you know what's good for you." A roar of laughter from the others filled the air as all their attentions were now focused on them. Patrick felt Ferdy tense as Florence stood riveted to the spot. Ferdy stood up slowly, his chains falling from his ankles clattering on to the ground as he stood. The clatter had gone unheard by his captors due to their loud laughter and ever increasing drunken state. Ferdy pushed Florence behind him and quickly dropped a key into Patrick's lap. "Quick, undo your chains we have to run." Patrick's look of wonder spurred Ferdy to quickly explain. "Don't worry they will all be feeling drowsy by now, I had given Florence a herb tincture to add to their ale and soon they will not be able to keep awake. Just be ready to run for your life." Almost before the last words had come out of this mouth, their captors started to sway, losing their footing. Gradually they started to fall to the ground, some less graceful than others. Ferdy winked at Patrick. "They don't know this land like me nor do they possess the knowledge of its fruits and herbs that it yields." With that they all took to their heels and ran, following Ferdy's lead.

Chapter Sixty-Seven

It seemed to Patrick that they had been running for hours before Ferdy stopped in order for them to take a breath. Although hardly being able to speak, he whispered, "Over there," as he pointed to a small opening in one of the caves that was now in front of them. They all started running again until they reached the mouth of the cave. It was only then that Patrick noticed for the first time what looked like a small pyramid to the left of the cave. He had no time to gather his thoughts, as he mustered up the last of his strength to almost throw himself into the cave's welcome shelter. It was dark inside but not cold, offering a sense of calm as they all just stopped to catch their breath.

He felt Ferdy's hand on his shoulder asking him if he was alright. He managed to nod his head as his breathing gradually became slower after the exertion of their escape. Ferdy smiled at him. "We will be safe here for a while, I know these caves well and the land surrounding it. We will wait until dark and then head back to my village. It is time that we stopped these barbarians." Ferdy's brow furrowed with anger showing his emotions as he spoke. Florence, who had been silent in the shadows, came forward and slipped her hand into Ferdy's. At this point a great sense of wellbeing suddenly overcame Patrick and a surety that this was the beginning of change and that he, along with Ferdy and Florence would be important in these times of change. The path would not be easy but strength and courage would win through the dark times that lay ahead. Patrick realised that this was why he was being shown this brief glimpse into a past life and as this realisation dawned, he began to feel dizzy; the faces of Ferdy and Florence going in and out of focus. He knew that their Patrick would remain with them to carry that life role but he was being pulled back, the dark cave disappearing in front of his eyes as light filled its space. The events which took place after they had escaped, playing out before him, like a film on fast play. He had experienced that beginning again to give him courage and hope for the future and he felt calm and at peace.

He was now once again back on the peaceful shores of Kerry feeling the warmth of the sun caressing his body. All the feelings of distress ebbing away from him, his body which had been battered and bruised, healed. He could faintly hear Admar's voice calling to him to return but he didn't want to go back yet, instead he looked out over the shoreline and with such clarity he knew who he was, his purpose, what he had achieved in the past and what lay ahead in the future. He wanted to remain in this peaceful bubble of space for a little longer but Admar's voice was getting clearer and louder, knowing that it would not be long before he had to return. Ferdy and Florence would be OK, they would help to change the culture of that time, their bond would be strengthened and their love so intense that eventually they would return again as Joshua and Torri in another time with an even greater role to play. He had recognised them straight away, even though a different guise and in a different time. Who they were was so clear to Patrick, they were all linked together. Braedan too was linked to them and would fulfil his destiny with the help of all those that would grow to love him. At this moment he saw all that was and would be before the memories started to leave him.

Such was his desire to stay in this special place it was with some sadness that he succumbed to the pleas from Admar to return, the dizziness overwhelming him as the beautiful landscape disappeared, followed by silence as his eyes opened again to the smiling face of Admar and the concerned look of Megan, who was so pleased that he had woken that she gave him such a hug that he could hardly breathe, making him smile. They all looked at each other in silence.

Chapter Sixty-Eight

The silence that had surrounded them was suddenly broken by shouts from outside the cave. It was Braedan, he had returned.

The commotion and the urgency of Braedan's shouts had everyone running to the cave's entrance as quickly as possible. Braedan had Olivia in his arms, struggling against the extreme winds and driving rain, which a man of lesser strength would not have been able to bear. Josh and Patrick quickly ran to his aid, Patrick lifting Olivia's small battered body from Braedan's arms and taking her quickly into the cave to enable Josh to help him into safety. Megan and Torri rushed over to offer whatever help they could and Patrick looked over at Torri who was pointing over to another part of the cave which looked like it had a passageway joined to it. "Come, follow me, this leads into the pyramid where you will all be safe. There is a place for each of you to rest until the time is right."

There were no questions; they all immediately followed letting Josh and Torri lead the way, trusting in them completely. They walked through a narrow passageway. Patrick realised it was the same way Josh and Torri had entered the cave when he had first seen them. As they walked further, deeper into the passageway, the dark stone from which the cave was made was gradually being replaced with a lighter substance and the passageway was wider although surprisingly long. The light now became quite strong as the passageway broadened out. The end of the tunnel revealed a triangular shaped door opening out into a hexagonal shaped chamber. The chamber was well lit and they each felt that they were being physically embraced by its warmth, all feeling completely safe within its realm. This time Josh spoke. "The Pyramid of Life will keep us all safe and Torri and I will watch over you as you sleep. Many will flourish in the caves for many years as there is still some time for the Earth before its change. We shall be watching over you now and for the time that is to come."

They all remained silent with no questions as four pod-like vessels opened up from within the walls of the chamber. Braedan who had been carrying Olivia again, laid her down gently into the first pod and watched to ensure that Patrick and Megan got safely into theirs. Satisfied that they were all safe, he climbed into the last pod. The last thing he saw was Evia smiling at him and then darkness. The pods gently engulfed each body with its essence before taking them into its heart to begin a new continuum of life, the symbols and DNA codes ready within it, to ensure that life would be ready for the new world.

Josh turned to Admar and smiled. "I know that it is your time to go home and that Torri and I will be able to exist in our protective vibration as you have for so many thousands of years. Nothing can harm us as we watch the new world taking form. We will miss seeing you but we will always be able to feel your presence. We have much work to do but time is limitless."

Evia wrapped her arms around Torri and then Josh, not having to say any words. Their time now done, they could return home to rest. They faded away slowly as Josh and Torri watched with both sadness and happiness, witnessing their final journey home.

Chapter Sixty-Nine

Jupiter's red gas spot glowed almost angrily, brighter than ever before and clearly visible by the naked eye, not restricted to the night sky but could be seen even during the brightness of the daylight sky. Many years ago this would have caused major interest and speculation, even concern but now there was no one to witness it. Changes in solar patterns and planetary positions had happened slowly at first but now these changes were accelerating. Jupiter, the giant planet of the solar system, had protected the Earth and many of the other planets by consuming meteors and objects which would have otherwise caused destruction and devastation. It had more than earned its name as the protector planet of our solar system given to it by ancient astronomers. With its size it was so close to being a star in its own right, its magnetic field provided its 63 moons with their own mini solar system. One of the last missions sent to Jupiter in 2011, was the Juno probe, which was at a time when man still had a thirst for knowledge and adventure. The probe had discovered much about Jupiter but this knowledge had been forgotten and now provoked little interest. The project and its organisation long abandoned through lack of money and interest at the time. The true nature of Jupiter, however, had not been discovered nor of that of the pyramids and their close connection with life and its creation. Jupiter's mass of burning gases would give no cause to think that deep within its burning liquid it was nurturing new planets, forming them ready to replace the old and giving them form before their birth into space. This was the case with Europa, observed as one of Jupiter's moons for many hundreds of years and known for the possibilities of having its own oceans. Time had run out on human research and no more had been discovered. So much information had been lost or consumed by T.R.I.G.O.M. that it had not been generally available. The Earth would soon be moving into its last stage of life, before its release from the life force of the pyramid. A new Epoch would begin again but of a different origin and a different path. The oxygen that had provided life was growing less and the shift in the Earth's spin meant that those who remained on the planet would struggle to survive through its remaining years. Ultimately the human body would need to evolve to survive another age, a new planet of a different structure. D.N.A. for this transformation had been kept safe within the symbols of the ancients. Their secrets kept safe until the force within the pyramid activated their use, the destiny already written for those that had been chosen and for the two that would be always there to witness and nurture new life. Providing clues of past existence to new life to interpret into whatever they can imagine but leaving another mystery perhaps just out of their grasp as had been done before. They could even evolve to solve the clues and ascend to a higher level. The opportunities had always been there for all past existences but few had even begun to brush the surface. However not all knowledge was meant to be found but instead remain just out of reach to provoke a journey of discovery and to search within for something perhaps more important than the secrets of the universe.

Chapter Seventy

Josh and Torri held hands as they looked out from the mouth of cave which was preserved in its appearance, protected from harm through its connection to the pyramid, the Star of Life. Josh and Torri looked as young as they had been when they had first entered the Great Pyramid. They had stood together, looking out, many times as they had done so from the start of the great change. The five thousand years that had passed were nothing in the scale of time. They had frequently walked to the mouth of the cave to observe, protected from harm within their vibration, witnessing its transformation, before returning back to their own dimension within the pyramid. They took the same route through the passageways which the pyramid had created to allow them to witness the formation of the new world that they would watch over. It had been like watching an embryo growing in its mother's womb; the beauty of creation, this time a new world. The wonder and pleasure of being able to see it forming was beyond any words that they could utter. The pyramid standing in all its glory, its force physically emanating around the new planet as it formed around it. Watching this wonder brought such joy but they also felt the sadness and even grief for the Earth which had sustained life for so long. It had been such a beautiful planet, home to all manner of creation. The Earth had now taken its place amongst the other lights in the sky, its purpose fulfilled but remained observable, like Mars had done to the Earth's occupants when they had first walked upon its surface. The last remaining humans had dwelt on the Earth for a further few hundred years after the destruction of T.R.I.G.O.M. Ironically, the skills and knowledge that human kind had achieved over many thousands of years, leading to the creation of T.R.I.G.O.M. had then had a reverse effect. They had stopped learning and exploring for themselves, forgetting the knowledge that had once made them great and dominant over all species. They had been complacent, losing the thirst for life, just content to leave the technology that they had initially created to think for them and to cater for all their needs. When the source of their dependency had been suddenly taken away from them, the extent of this degradation was exposed. In the last years of humanity upon the Earth, life had reverted back to the beginning. Just like early man, they had inhabited the local caves, recording these events by word of mouth and childlike drawings. Before Braedan returned to Patrick and the others, he had instructed the Hubot to find as many people as possible. He made sure it would lead them to the protection of the caves where they would find shelter within them. Although this had been many years ago before the Earth was no more, this story had been passed down to each generation. The story slightly changed with each generation that followed and ultimately depicted in one of the caves, in their own form of wall art. Here the Hubot was shown as a huge glowing giant, with a halo of light leading their ancestors to safety. They had called it the shining one and some had even built a shrine to pay tribute for their salvation. They had survived with just basic knowledge and primal instincts. When the time had come, they had all perished quickly, not knowing what was happening. The Earth was released from the life force of the pyramid to take its new place and orbit around the Sun. Their spirits released and their bodies destroyed as the planet succumbed to its own release of molten lava, its oxygen being sucked away and hot poisonous gases increasing to take their hold. The seas long vanished and the last drop of life-giving liquid, rising up and evaporating, lost forever. The once blue planet was no more, now glowing red in the blackness of space.

Josh and Torri did not dwell too much on this loss; they knew that nothing was lost and a new world would be host to all. This special cave would be the entrance for the first dwellers of this new world and from which they would enter and explore their new home. It only had the appearance of a cave but in reality it was an extension of the Life Star, the pyramid which protected it for all time, a one way passage for new life on a new world. It was their connection to this new world and to their own dimension, so that they could always be there. Josh and Torri had not stood at the mouth of the cave to look out for some time. It could have been hundreds of years to this new world, their time was different and what was just a few hours to them, was decades here. Knowing that it was almost ready, the turbulence of its forming abated and its beauty ready to be unveiled, Josh took Torri's hand. They stepped to the edge of the cave, which had a small ledge, wide enough to stand on and look out. They were ready to see for the first time this world as it would appear to the first forms of life.

From this moment they would look out on to a new world, the first to see it before new life would be introduced to it. This planet would be like a blank canvas for new life to write their story, to record their achievements on their path of evolution. Joshua and Torri would not know the outcome that this new Epoch of life would bring. They had only limited knowledge as to the blueprint of this world and even with the new knowledge that they now possessed, they too would be learning along the way. They would only be able to intervene should they be called upon to do so. They knew that they would never be alone in this task and could always seek guidance within the pyramid and be energised by the light that passed through it. At times when this transformation had just started to take place, they had often looked up into the dark skies and had taken comfort in the brightness of the stars. There was a bright halo around one of the new moons that circled this new planet. Admar and Evia were still with them and always would be.

They had both got their eyes closed as they stood, completely silent, time standing still for them until they were ready for a moment that would never be experienced by them again and so now they were ready ...

Epilogue

Their eyes closed but their minds as one, Josh and Torri reflected on this great moment in time. The new dawn was approaching and as the cave men had emerged on to the Earth so many millennia ago, a new form of life would do the same. Beings with no memories of other lives, other worlds. Beings with free will to choose their own path, to evolve, just as the first humans had done so. The pyramid would still be in all its glory, perhaps like it had been in the time that the Earth had first formed around it. It would be a structure to puzzle over, to try and find out where it had come from or who had built it. This gift from the stars would be the only connection to past life and a past world. Would new life advance enough to discover its secrets? Would they be impelled by knowledge or would they choose to regress as human kind had done? Such opportunities lay ahead with millions of years for its process. However, as they both knew, the time for this planet to remain within the force of the pyramid was not infinite but the time it had would measure the advancement of the next physical beings. Their markings would join the others on the face of the pyramid. This purpose had not been clear to Admar and Evia, nor was it clear to Joshua and Torri. They only knew that one day they would matter.

The time now had come. As they opened their eyes, they both gasped, the new world; the new time was before them and amongst all its glory, shining so bright was the pyramid, glowing with its life force and ensuring the continuum of life. So it begins …

The author

In Symbols of the Future, the debut novel of
Caroline Read, inspiration is drawn from her
interest in the planets and a love of the stories of
E.M. Forster.

Born and bred in Nottingham, Caroline is well-
known locally for her poetry and this success has
driven her writing towards her thought-provoking
and entertaining first novel.

The publisher

Whoever stops getting better, will in time stop being good.

This is the motto of novum publishing, and our focus is on finding new manuscripts, publishing them and offering long-term support to the authors.
Our publishing house was founded in 1997, and since then it has become THE expert for new authors and has won numerous awards.

Our editorial team will peruse each manuscript within a few weeks free of charge and without obligation.

You will find more information about
novum publishing and our books on the internet:

w w w . n o v u m - p u b l i s h i n g . c o . u k

Printed in Great Britain
by Amazon